A NEW BEGINNING

JUDITH A. PERKINS

EXPLORA BOOKS
700 – 838 West Hastings St. Vancouver, BC V6C 0A6
www.explorabooks.com
Phone: (604) 330 6795

ISBN: 978-1-997587-25-5 (Paperback)
978-1-997587-26-2 (eBook)

A NEW BEGINNING

JUDITH A. PERKINS

Table of Contents

CHAPTER 1

On August 1, 1939, George Taylor was trying very hard to celebrate his 39th birthday with his wife and son, but times were hard and he wasn't in a very good mood to celebrate. He and Gladys, his wife, and Peter, his son, were living on his in-laws' farm, trying to produce a crop that they could sell, but the land and the weather were not cooperating with them. It was hot and dry, and there was no water in the creek to irrigate the crops. They just withered and died in the ground.

"I don't know where we are going to come up with the money to pay our debts. We owe the bank for the mortgage on this farm, we owe Sam for groceries and feed for the animals, and we owe Doc Pederson for setting Peter's broken arm last year," George explained to Gladys.

"Daddy, I can go to work," Peter said to his father.

"No, son! You have to go to school. There is no hope at all unless you get a good education. Anyway, I need your help around here," George stated.

"I don't want you working for someone else, Peter," Gladys said. "You might get hurt again and I wouldn't know about it." Gladys was very protective of Peter. Both she and George came from large families, but Peter was her only child and she was not able to have any more. She kept a very close eye on him. She wasn't happy that he would be going into town for school each day. She wanted him home with her, but George insisted. He knew that Peter would have a bleak future without a good education and that started with the first grade.

Elias Sheen was the president of the bank in the town of Memphis. He was a kind man and had great empathy for all of the people who were struggling with the effects of the Depression, but he had superiors that he had to report to, and they wanted their money. Most of the farmers were in trouble because of the drought and their inability to bring in a crop, and most of them were in arrears on their mortgage payments. Elias had some serious decisions to make about the disposition of those loans. He had a pile of files on his desk, the loans that were the oldest on the top. He was working his way down the pile.

George and Gladys knew that their file was somewhere on Elias' desk. George had been in to see him last month to ask for an extension on the loan payment. Elias had given it to him but warned him that it couldn't happen again. He needed some good faith payment to extend any longer.

George had sold just about everything that had any value on the farm. All he had left was his car. It was a 1929 Model A Ford, and he was not about to give that up. Besides his wife and son, he loved that car the most. He did not drive it often as he had no money for parts or gasoline. Other than the car, George and Gladys had nothing else to sell. Gladys did have her mother's engagement ring put away for Peter someday. She did not want to sell it. It was her one treasure, but it was getting to the point where they had to have the money or lose the farm. Then what would they do? They had nowhere else to go.

One day, when George was out in the field plowing under the stubble of a crop that did not grow, Gladys took the ring out of her special box in her dresser drawer, put it into her purse, and started walking the three miles to town. Gladys walked into the bank and approached Elias Sheen's desk.

"Hello, Mrs. Taylor. What can I do for you?" he asked.

"What will you give me for this ring?" she asked him as she put the ring on his desk.

Elias picked up the ring and looked at it. He was becoming quite the expert on the value of jewelry. People had been giving him different pieces of jewelry in exchange for payment on their loans for several years now. He was pretty good about assessing the value of different items.

"I can give you $45.00 for this ring, Gladys. Are you sure you want to sell it?" he asked.

"No. I do not want to sell it, but we have no choice. We must pay our debts. If you give me $45.00 for the ring and I make a $25.00 payment on our mortgage loan, will that buy us some time to find the rest?" she asked in a pleading voice.

"Yes. I can give you another six months to pay the balance."

"All right. Please give me the difference of $20.00 in five dollar bills. I have some other bills that need to be paid," Gladys requested.

After the transaction was complete at the bank, Gladys went to the general store to see Sam Roberts. "Hello, Sam. How are you today?" Gladys asked.

"I am fine, Gladys. What can I do for you today?" he asked.

"I am here to pay $5.00 on our grocery bill and $5.00 on our feed bill. I know that we owe more than that, but I am hoping this amount will buy a little time for us to come up with the rest," Gladys explained to Sam.

"That will be fine, Gladys. Any payment is greatly appreciated," Sam said.

"Thank you. Have a good day," Gladys said as she was leaving the store.

Gladys walked home slowly, thinking about the ring that she would never see again. That ring being in her dresser drawer gave her a feeling of closeness to her mother. She was sad that she had to give up the ring, but glad that she was able to give George the relief of not being so stressed about money. After the six months, she wasn't sure what she would do. Maybe things in the country would be better by then. She certainly hoped so.

When Gladys told George about selling her mother's ring, he felt very bad for her, but he was relieved to have a little more time to figure out how he was going to support his family.

"Thank you, my dear. I know how much that ring meant to you. Now we have a little time to figure out what we are going to do," George said to Gladys.

Once a week, George would go into town to pick up his mail at the post office. They did not have mail delivery to their farm. It was a social time for George, and he was able to talk to a lot of his neighbors and catch up on the happenings around the area.

When he went into the post office to pick up his mail, he had a letter from his brother Dan. Dan and his wife Emma lived in a small town in Washington near the ocean. Dan owned a Texaco Oil Distributorship in Raymond, WA. Dan and Emma had no children, but lived a full and busy life in Raymond.

George was surprised to hear from him. Dan was not one to write a lot of letters. Emma occasionally wrote to let the family know what was going on in their lives, but that was not often.

George sat on a bench in the city park and opened the letter to see what Dan had to say. When he opened the letter, he found a check for $600.00. George had never seen that much money at one time in his life. He read the letter.

"Dear George and Gladys, I hope that all is well with you and Peter. We are doing fine here in Raymond, but George, I have a problem that I could use your help with. As you know, I have a Texaco service station here in town, and I am having a very hard time finding someone to run it for me. I am busy at the plant and cannot be running to the station every time there is a problem. I need someone I can trust to take the helm. And I think that someone is you. I know that you are having a hard time keeping the farm going. It is difficult for everyone who is trying to farm the land now," Dan wrote. "George, I would like to offer you a job as the manager of my filling station. You are the only one I know in whom I can trust with my business. I am sending you a check to cover the cost of settling your outstanding debts and to make the trip to Washington. What say, brother? Will you help me out? Write back to me as soon as you can with your decision. If you choose not to come, think of the $600.00 as a part of your inheritance from us.

Our love and best to you, Dan and Emma."

George sat on the bench and was in shock. He held in his hands the answer to his prayers. The money that Dan had sent would pay the outstanding mortgage amount, pay the feed and grocery bills, and pay Doc Pederson, and give them enough money to drive to Raymond, WA and start a new life. The biggest question would be whether Gladys would be willing to leave the farm and move clear across the country. $100.00 a month was almost impossible to turn down, especially during this awful Depression.

George got up and walked to where his car was parked. He stood beside it, looking and trying to figure out how they would get everything they would need to take with them into that vehicle and drive it to Washington State, an area neither of them had ever been to and neither of them knew anything about. But his brother had just given him a lifeline. Enough money to pay off his debts and to get them there, and a job earning $100.00 a month. That was unheard of.

Would Gladys want to go? Would she be willing to uproot her life and Peter's life to move to a place that was totally foreign to her? And would she be willing to live with the fact that he had lost her family's farm? He would only be able to pay off the back mortgage payments. He would have to give the farm to the bank, and they would be out from under the burden of the payments. George put the letter along with the check into his shirt pocket and drove home.

As he pulled into the driveway beside the house, Peter came running out, hollering, "Any mail for me, Dad?"

"Not this time, son," George answered. "But we did get a letter from your Uncle Dan in Washington."

"Your brother, Dad?" Peter asked excitedly.

"Yeah, my brother," said George. "Let's go inside, and I will read it to you and Mama," George said as he let Peter into the kitchen.

"We got a letter from Uncle Dan, Mama. He lives in Washington," shouted Peter. "Dad's going to read it to us. Sit down, Mama. Please sit down."

Gladys looked at George with a surprised look, wiped her hands on a dish towel, and sat down at the table. "What is it, George?" she asked nervously.

George sat down and proceeded to read the letter to both of them. Gladys was muttering that they couldn't move way out there. As far as she was concerned, that was Indian Territory. She wasn't going to put her son in danger by going there. "We can't afford to move there, George. How would we get there?" Just then, George put the check for $600.00 on the table in front of her. Gladys looked at it in awe. "I have never seen that much money at once," she whispered as she held the check in her hands.

"What is it, Dad?" Peter asked. "That doesn't look like money."

"This is called a check, Peter. We can take it to Mr. Sheen at the bank, and he will give us the money for it," George explained.

"Uncle Dan and Aunt Emma are asking us to move to their home in Raymond, Washington. Uncle Dan has a job for me in his filling station. We have to decide whether we are going to take the job and move away from here."

"Would Champ be able to move to Washington too?" Peter asked.

"I will have to write to Dan and find out if the invitation includes Champ, but I am pretty sure that would be okay. Dan likes dogs," George assured his son.

"Okay, Dad. I'm going out to play with Champ now," Peter announced as he ran out, letting the screen door slam behind him.

"What do you think, Gladys?" George asked his wife.

"I am afraid. I have never been away from here, and we would lose this farm, wouldn't we?" she asked.

"Yes. We would lose the farm. This is enough money to pay off our outstanding debts, but not enough to pay the complete loan off. We would have to forfeit the farm to the bank. As much as I hate doing that, I don't see that we have any choice. Dan is offering us a lifeline here with a job at a salary of $100.00 a month. There is nothing even close to that around here. There is no chance to have a decent crop to harvest with the land and the weather the way they are now. I can only see things getting worse and us without a roof over our heads," George explained.

"How would we get there?" asked Gladys quietly.

"If we are very careful, we can drive. I have a feeling we will need the car there. We would live with Dan and Emma for a while and get our own place as soon as we can afford one. I know you don't know Emma well, but it will work out fine. I don't see any other way for us," George said firmly.

"It frightens me to leave here. This is all I have ever known, but I agree with you. There is no future here for us, and Peter needs better than this," she conceded.

"I will need to talk to Elias at the bank and see if, by paying the past due amount, he will allow us to stay here until the spring. I would not want to start a trip west until then. It will be a very educational trip for Peter. Actually, for all of us," George explained.

Elias was surprised that the Taylors were going to pay their past due amount and sorry that they would be leaving the area. He agreed that they should not start the trip until the spring and made an arrangement with George to do some work on the house and barn to make it more saleable. Elias did not really want the property, but if the Taylors were going to leave, the place might as well be as presentable as possible. He knew that Gladys was a very good housekeeper and the house would be in immaculate condition. He also knew that George was meticulous about his equipment and the way the yard looked. Not having the Taylors as part of their community would be a loss. The family had been here for a very long time. The Taylors and McCreatys, Gladys' parents, had been some of the first settlers in the area, and now they would all be gone.

CHAPTER 2

Peter went back to school in September. He turned eight years old in August and was in the second grade. He was doing average work, but really excelled in sports. He loved to play softball during recess and was a very good runner. He was large for his age, and Gladys was forever remaking old clothes for him. She was going to take $2.00 and order him some new clothes from the Sears, Roebuck catalog.

George spent the fall months getting the fields cleaned and neatly plowed. He was not going to plant a crop in the spring because he would not be here to harvest it, but he wanted to have the fields neat and tidy. He did plant some winter vegetables in the kitchen garden for them to eat in the spring. They would probably eat some of their chickens in the spring before they left. "Before they left" was a phrase that both George and Gladys said quite often. Everything seemed to be based on when they left.

Thanksgiving and Christmas were quiet. They had a few gifts for Peter but did not want a lot more to pack. They were going to be limited on space as it was. They could take only what they could pack in the car. George was figuring out how he was going to get everything that they needed into or on top of the car.

January 1st brought a new decade and the promise of a new life for the Taylor family. George was getting ready to paint the inside of the house. A new coat of paint would make the house look so much better.

"I am going to do some repairs on the kitchen cupboards before I paint in there. I do need you to put the dishes and pots and pans and other stuff into boxes sooner than I thought. Can you work out of boxes for a while?" George asked Gladys.

"Yes, I can manage. Everything will need to be packed anyway. I will have to pick and choose what I want to take. We will be living with Dan and Emma for a while, so I will not need them until we have our own place. I am nervous about living in the same house as Emma. I do not know her well," Gladys added.

"Things will work out," George said confidently.

George and Gladys made the decision to leave Missouri on the 14th of April. George thought that the weather would be favorable for a trip across country in April. He also thought that it would take them about two weeks to make the trip from Memphis, Missouri, to Raymond, Washington. Thanks to Dan, if they were very careful, they would have enough money to make the trip.

By the end of March 1940, the papers were signed at the bank, and the farm would be relinquished as of the 14th of April. Neighbors and friends from town were in and out of their house during the last two weeks saying goodbye. Peter was excited to get on the road. Every day, he would check to see how much longer it would be before they packed up the car and left.

George completed the necessary repairs on the house and barn and two of the outbuildings. He dug a new hole so he could move the outhouse. He was going to have to do that in another few months anyway, so he decided to do it before they left. He was sure Elias would appreciate the effort.

Gladys was busy in the house, making sure everything was clean and in order. She packed all of her dishes in sturdy wooden boxes. The few clothes that the three of them had were put into two small satchels. Anything that didn't fit Peter went to the clothes box at their church. There was one chair that Gladys insisted get into the car. It was her Papa's chair. George groaned at the thought of taking it, but managed to fit it on the top of the car along with most of the boxes.

Finally, the day came that they finished putting the rest of their belongings into the car. George had tied what he could to the top and put a canvas over everything. It was a good thing that only the three of them were traveling. They couldn't have squeezed one more person into the Model A. George filled two canvas bags with water and hung them on the front bumper of the car so that they would have enough water to fill the radiator when needed. Gladys had prepared some snacks for them, and neighbors had given them bits of food to take with them. After tearful goodbyes from friends at church and their neighbors, they left Memphis, Missouri, and headed west. George and Peter were excited about going on a new adventure. Gladys was so scared that she could hardly move.

They had almost 2,000 miles to drive to get to Dan and Emma's house. George had done the calculations and thought that if they drove about 250 miles a day, they could get there in eight days. He would probably have to do most of the driving, especially when they hit the mountains. He had heard from others that the roads through the mountains could be treacherous. He knew that Gladys would be scared to death. She would be willing to drive through Missouri and Kansas, but once they got to the Rocky Mountains, she would not be able to even look out the window.

"Dad, where are we going to sleep?" Peter asked as they were getting towards the end of the first day.

"I thought that we would set up a camp someplace along the side of the road and we could build a fire to heat some food and maybe sleep in the car. We have three bedrolls with us to sleep out under the stars," George answered his son.

Gladys interjected, "I will sleep in the car. You and your dad can sleep out under the stars. I will be just as happy to stay in the car."

"Are you afraid, Mama?" asked Peter.

"You bet I am," answered Gladys. "I am not ready to come in contact with some wild animal that wants to eat me."

"Oh, Mom! We won't see any wild animals," Peter exclaimed.

"I'm not so sure about that," Gladys commented.

George was laughing at the conversation between mother and son. The only problem was that he knew she really was scared. She was terrified of taking this trip. She didn't want to leave the farm, but they had no choice. She had begged and begged for George to find some other solution to their financial problems. She did not want to leave northern Missouri. It was the only place she had ever lived, and every friend she ever had was still there.

Gladys had tears in her eyes most of the first day on the road. She kept turning around and looking back, but George was only looking forward. The thought of a job that would pay him a decent salary, not breaking his back trying to plow land that was dry and used up, and being with his family was a lure he could not resist. The possibilities for Peter were endless. He would have a chance to get a decent education and make something of himself.

"Gladys, would you like to drive for a while?" George asked his wife.

"No. These roads are unfamiliar to me, and I would feel uncomfortable driving on them," Gladys stated firmly.

"Okay. If you are not going to help drive, it is going to take us a few days longer to get there. I cannot drive without some rest time," George shot back, trying to be as nice and gentle as possible and not upset Peter with an argument between his parents.

"You are the one who decided to move away. You are the one who will have to do the driving," she almost shouted at George.

By this time, they had been on the road almost four hours. They had stopped for a bathroom break and to fill the car with gasoline, but that was only for about 15 minutes, and George had no chance to rest. He pulled over to the side of the road, turned the car off, and got out of the car. He walked around to make sure everything was tied down and secure, then he got back into the car, leaned his head back, and closed his eyes.

"What are you doing? It is the middle of the day. You cannot go to sleep now," Gladys exclaimed.

"If you want me to fall asleep while I am driving, or if you will not help with the driving, you will be patient and let me rest for an hour," George mumbled.

Peter was sitting in the back seat, trying to ignore the exchange between his parents. He had been listening to them bicker for a few weeks now and had gotten used to blocking them out.

"Oh, for heaven's sake," Gladys said as she got out of the car and walked around to the driver's side. She opened the door and said, "Get out. I will drive. We cannot sit along the side of the road every time you decide to take a nap."

George got out, smiled at his wife, kissed her on the forehead, and said, "Thank you, dear."

Gladys drove for about two hours without saying anything to George. George did not sleep but rested with his eyes closed. Every once in a while, he would ask her if she was doing okay. Gladys would just mumble something that he could not hear or understand, and he would close his eyes again.

All this time, Peter was sitting in the back seat smiling. His dad sure had a way with his mom.

By 2:00 o'clock in the afternoon, they were approaching St. Joseph, Mo. They had stopped at a roadside rest stop along the way and had a bite to eat for lunch about noon, but George wanted to keep going for a while. Kansas City, Kansas, was only 52 miles south. St. Joseph was where George wanted to turn west to drive through Kansas and Colorado. This second night, he thought he would give Gladys a treat and stay in a hotel if he could find one that wasn't bug-infested and wouldn't use up all the money in his pocket.

The family stayed in an old but clean hotel on the west side of Kansas City that second night. Gladys thoroughly enjoyed staying in a hotel and letting everyone else clean up after her. George had to remind her that she did not have to make the bed in the morning. The maids would put clean sheets on it for the next person to stay there. As they were eating breakfast, George was listening to conversations around him. People were talking about the road conditions going through the mountains. They were saying that the roads were still icy and some were still covered with snow. Maybe he should think about changing their route to go through Wyoming. They would still have to go through some mountainous terrain, but maybe not as bad as Colorado.

"Dear, I was listening to some of the people in the restaurant talking about the road conditions in the mountains of Colorado. It is still icy, and some of the roads still have snow on them. I am thinking that we should change our route to go through Nebraska and Wyoming. It might take us another day or two, but it could save some trouble on icy roads," George explained to Gladys. "We would still have to go through some mountains, but maybe not as bad as the Rockies. What do you think?"

"I am still scared, but that sounds a little better than before," Gladys answered.

George recalculated their mileage and route and decided that Nebraska and Wyoming were the way to go, so they turned northwest from St. Joseph and headed for Lincoln, Nebraska.

The car was running a little hot, and George had to stop fairly often to check the water in the radiator. Fortunately, they were driving alongside a river and had easy access to water. Each one of them had a canteen for drinking water, and they had the two canvas bags full of water for the radiator. It was Peter's job to make sure that the bags were filled after putting water into the radiator.

George knew that they would not be able to stay in a hotel every night and would have to camp out. Gladys wasn't happy about it and had been adamant that she was going to sleep in the car. Peter was excited about camping out.

The third night out, the Taylors made it to 25 miles past Lincoln, Nebraska, when they decided to stop for the night. They found a roadside camping area that was along a stream. George and Peter got their fishing poles out of the back of the car and went to the water to catch their dinner. Even before Gladys had the fire going and the frying pan out, they had caught four very nice trout. With the fish, along with some biscuits saved from breakfast that morning, they had a feast. George and Peter settled down in their packs beside the fire, and Gladys retired to the front seat of the car with her coat and two blankets.

After a restless night for all three of them, they washed up in the cold stream, packed up the car, and headed west. George explained to both Peter and Gladys that if they were going to have enough money to make it to Washington, they would have to camp out more nights than they stayed in hotels. They had to have a reserve of money for gasoline and any possible repairs that would be needed on the car. They would also have to purchase food, so they had to be careful.

CHAPTER 3

George and Peter were enjoying the ride through Nebraska. The land was very similar to Missouri: flat and very dry. There was nothing growing on the land, just a bit of scrub. They could see farmers out in the fields plowing under what vegetation there was, getting ready to try and grow a crop for the late spring and summer. George was glad he didn't have to do that anymore. It was backbreaking work with little reward for the effort.

From Lincoln, they drove to North Platte, then into Wyoming. After camping for three nights, George thought it was about time to get a hotel room, have a nice bath, and sleep in a bed. When they arrived in Cheyenne, he found a hotel with a room available and a bathtub down the hall with plenty of hot water. The only problem was that it was noisy all night. There was a tavern next door to the hotel, and being a Friday night, all of the farm hands came into town for their weekly entertainment. Gladys was embarrassed at the language used and was concerned about Peter hearing what was being said. George just laughed. After about one o'clock in the morning, George and Gladys managed to get some sleep. It was nine o'clock on Saturday morning before they finished eating some breakfast and got on the road.

"George, we are going to have to be more careful where we stay from now on. I was very concerned about what Peter was listening to," Gladys complained.

"I couldn't hear anything, Mama. I was asleep," Peter told her.

"Well, I certainly don't know how you slept through all that noise," Gladys said.

From Cheyenne, the Taylors drove into Indian country. After leaving Cheyenne, they drove through the Crow Indian Reservation.

"Are those men walking along the road Indians, Dad?" Peter asked.

"They probably are. Most Indians, no matter what tribe they belong to, have black hair, and the men wear it long," George answered.

"They are not going to hurt us, are they?" Gladys asked with a hint of fear in her voice.

George looked at her for a minute, surprised at her question. "Of course not," he stated firmly. "Indians are not savages."

"The books say they are, Dad," Peter said.

"The books were written a long, long time ago, and many of those books are fiction anyway, not true stories. One of the things that is not written about a lot is how we took the Indians' land away from them," George said.

"How could we take land away from them, Dad?" Peter asked.

"The white man moved west and settled on the land that belonged to the Indians, and the government let them. We broke the treaties we had with them and forcibly moved them onto reservations where they could not roam free like they did before," George explained.

"Where did you learn all this, Dad?" Peter asked.

"I read it in books. Even though I only went to school through the 10th grade, I continued to read. You know I love to read books," George replied.

"Yes, I know. You always have your nose in a book," Peter laughed.

"That is surely a fact!" asserted Gladys.

All three of them were laughing when they heard a clunking sound coming from the rear of the car. George pulled over to the side of the road and got out to see what the problem was. He discovered a flat tire on the left rear side of the car.

"Sorry, but we are going to have to empty part of the car to get at the spare tire. Thank goodness I bought a new spare before we left home," George said.

After unloading, changing the tire, and reloading the car, it was time for some lunch, so they just stayed there and ate the sandwiches that they had purchased at the diner that morning.

"We are not far from Rawlins, Wyoming. We will stop there and get the tire fixed. We have to have a good spare," George mentioned.

After a 50-cent fix of the spare tire in Rawlins, they drove on to a nice camping area about 50 miles west of there. They had seen a lot of Indians walking along the road. Peter was fascinated by them, George thought them handsome people, and Gladys was just plain scared of them. She was sure all three of them were going to be scalped during the night. She would not let Peter sleep outside with his dad. So, they all piled into the car, and none of them got very much sleep that night. George was grumpy the next morning with only a cold biscuit for breakfast and no hot coffee to drink. He was going to stop at the next diner he saw to get at least a cup of coffee.

Gladys was just grateful she was alive and that the Indians had not scalped her during the night.

George stopped at the next filling station to fill the car with gasoline and check the oil and water. The station had a coffee pot on a stove, and George asked if he could pay for a cup of coffee. The owner looked at him and then at the pot of coffee.

"We normally don't sell coffee, but I guess it would be okay. I can always make another pot for me and my wife," the owner said.

George poured coffee into his cup, took a sip gratefully, and gave the man a quarter for it. After paying for his gasoline and a quart of oil, he thanked the owner and left to return to the car.

George was aware that they were gaining in altitude. He knew they were going to get into the mountains soon and was concerned about how Gladys was going to react. She apparently wasn't aware of the terrain changing as they drove along. He could tell she was on edge because they were on the Indian reservation. She truly thought that they were in danger just driving through.

Gladys was a smart woman but honestly believed that the Indians were still savages. Over the years that they had been married, he realized that she was very superstitious about things she did not understand. She was not a reader and would not study or learn about things she did not understand. She would say that they did not concern her, so why did she need to know about them?

This is exactly why he wanted Peter to get the best education that he could. He wanted him to at least know where to find answers to situations he did not understand.

While they were driving, Peter was continually talking about the country they were passing through. He had many questions about the area and the Indians who were living there.

George pointed out a herd of antelope grazing in a field not far off the road. They had seen a few deer along the way, too. There were little towns spaced 20 or 30 miles apart and lots of makeshift tents and tarps set up with Indians selling their crafts. George did not stop at any of the sites. They couldn't afford to buy anything anyway.

As they drove up into the mountains, the weather was getting cooler, and George knew that they would have to plan on staying in a hotel for the next few nights. It would be too cold to sleep in the car. Gladys didn't mind that at all. She figured if she was inside a building, she would be safe.

"Hey, Dad, look out the window over here. There are all kinds of big deer alongside the road and out into the fields. What are they, Dad?" Peter asked.

"Those are elk. Aren't they beautiful?" George answered his son. "I have heard that elk meat is very tasty, sometimes better than beef," George mentioned. The elk were right alongside the road, and George was being very careful driving. He did not want one to suddenly step out onto the road in front of him. He did see a couple of them in the road ahead and hoped that they would move before he got to them. There was no way to get around them. He honked his horn a couple of times, and they finally moved enough so that he could drive around them. They certainly were not afraid of the car or the people in it. Again, Gladys was petrified at the size of the elk.

"How do you know so much about the animals that live here, Dad?" Peter asked.

"I have read about them, Peter. I like to read all different kinds of books. That is the way I learn new things. I am able to travel to a lot of different places by reading books about those places. Even if I can't be there in person, I feel like I am when I read. I want you to be able to do the same thing. Maybe your Uncle Dan will know if there is a library in the town of Raymond, WA. If so, we will get you a library card, and you can check out books. Maybe your new school will have a library also," George said to Peter.

"What do you think, Gladys? Would you like to have a library card so you can check out books?" George asked his wife.

"I don't care," Gladys mumbled. She was sitting, staring out the passenger side window, not really looking at anything. "I just want to go back home."

"You know we can't do that, honey. The farm is not ours anymore. It hasn't been ours for a long time. I am sorry that I lost it, but we just could not produce a crop to sell. There was no money to pay the mortgage," George said.

"We could have tried again," Gladys cried.

"Gladys, the land was not productive. There was no water to irrigate and no money to buy seed to plant. I couldn't do it by myself. All of the help has left the area. Dan offered us a job for more money per month than we made in all of last year. How could we turn that down? This is a fresh start for us," George exclaimed. "We had no choice but to leave."

"I know, but I still want to go home," she said.

"You are going to have to get used to this life. You cannot go home. There is no home there," George told her.

"Be happy, Mama," Peter said. "We are going to have fun. Look, there are some more of those elk. They sure are big."

"Mama, let's sing some songs. Maybe that will cheer you up," Peter said.

"Not now, Peter," she mumbled.

They drove further up into the mountains. The roads were good and clear of snow, but there was some alongside the road. Peter wanted to stop and play in it, but George wanted to continue to drive. Their speed had reduced a lot, and he wanted to get through to a town called Rock Springs. Because of the cold, they could not sleep in the car, so they had to get a hotel room. George was hoping they could find a cheap one with a diner close by. He wanted to get an early start in the morning and get through the rest of the mountains.

They were able to find a cheap but clean hotel room in Rock Springs and had a good dinner and breakfast the next morning.

The road kept going up and up. George was concerned about the car and whether it would make the summit. So far, it was okay, but he had to reduce his speed to 20 miles per hour, and they were not making very good time.

George was surprised by the terrain. They would climb, hit a summit, and descend. He thought that was the end of the mountainous region, but then they would start to climb again. They would hit a summit and descend again. This went on for miles. George was getting discouraged. He had a five-gallon can of gasoline tied to the side of the car in case they couldn't make it to the next filling station. So far, he hadn't had to use it, but looking at the map, he saw no towns ahead for many miles and probably would have to fill the tank with the reserved fuel. He hoped that he would find a town with a hotel to stay in for the night and to refill the gas can if necessary.

Gladys was sitting in the passenger seat with her hands gripped together and tears running down her cheeks. Even Peter was quiet for a change. George was beginning to question his decision to make this trip.

CHAPTER 4

They drove through a corner of Utah and into Idaho. George was amazed at the scenery but concerned about the distance to another town.

About 6:00 PM, they finally came to a filling station alongside the road. While the owner was filling the car with fuel, George asked if there was a hotel nearby. The owner said there was no hotel close, but he had a room in the back of the station that he would let them use for the night. He and his wife lived in a house behind the station.

"I would certainly appreciate the use of the room. It has been a long day, and all three of us are tired. Your generosity is greatly appreciated," George said as he paid the man for the gasoline and three sandwiches he had in a cooler in the station. He had some Coca-Colas in a cooler, and George bought three of them.

The station owner showed them to the back room, and they all thanked him again before going into the room. There was a mattress on the floor, a small table, and two straight-backed chairs. The room was fairly clean, and it had a heater. They were very grateful to be able to stay there for the night.

George moved the car around to the back of the station and got their bedrolls out along with some of their personal belongings. They ate their sandwiches and drank their cokes, then lay down on the mattress, and all three were asleep within a short time.

When George looked at the map the next morning, he checked the mileage to Boise, the capital of Idaho. It was almost 250 miles, and he felt they could make it that far. He wanted to treat Gladys to a nice hotel and a good dinner that evening.

Even though they were driving through mountains, the road was fairly good, and they were making good time. Gladys even agreed to drive for a while. There was a fairly straight stretch of road between Twin Falls and Mountain Home, and she felt that she could drive it easily. George noticed that her fingers were gripped tightly to the steering wheel, but he didn't say anything to her. He didn't want to upset her, and he was enjoying looking at the passing scenery. Peter was busy trying to read one of George's books but was having a hard time with some of the words and spelling them out for George to tell him what they said.

"Peter, why don't you pick out one of your books to read?" George asked. "You know what most of those words are."

"Yours are more interesting, Dad," he answered as he went back to reading and, in another minute, spelled out another word.

George just laughed at him, and soon Gladys was tired of driving and pulled over to the side of the road. She got out and walked around the car, and George checked the water in the radiator. He topped off the water, got into the driver's side, and drove on down the road.

As they were driving into Twin Falls, George heard a clunk under the hood. He pulled over to see if he could see anything wrong. As he got out of the car, he saw a dead rabbit alongside the road.

George thought to himself, "Well, thank God it was only a rabbit and it did not damage the car." George knew that if he had hit a larger animal, there could have been major damage to the car, and they would be stuck.

"George, what is wrong with the car? Why did you stop?" Gladys asked.

"I heard a clunk and thought something was wrong with the engine, but all is okay. I checked everything," George answered. He did not want to tell either Gladys or Peter that he had hit an animal. They were too sympathetic about animals and would have been very sad.

The family arrived in Boise about 5:00 PM, found a nice hotel for a reasonable price, got cleaned up, and went out to dinner. The restaurant was around the corner from the hotel, and the clerk at the hotel said they were known for their corned beef and cabbage. That appealed to all three of them.

There was a jar of sauce on the table that was not marked. George knew by the look and the smell what it was and realized that Peter had never tasted horseradish. Peter wanted to taste it, and George warned him to take just a tiny bit on the end of his spoon, but Peter took a whole spoonful and put it in his mouth before George or Gladys could stop him.

Peter's mouth and throat were burning, and there wasn't enough water in the entire restaurant to put the fire out. He had tears in his eyes. When his dinner arrived, he had a hard time eating it because of the fire in his mouth.

"Why didn't you tell me it was hot, Dad?" Peter gasped.

"I told you to take just a little bit on the end of your spoon. You were the one who took the whole spoonful," George answered.

After the experience with the horseradish, Peter vowed that he would be very careful before he tasted anything new.

All three of the Taylors were able to take baths before bed that night, and all three of them slept very well. The next morning, they donned their last set of clean clothes, packed up their things, and loaded the car. After paying the bill and thanking the clerk for the recommendation of the restaurant last night, they climbed into the car and took off for Washington.

George looked at the map carefully before he left Boise and realized that he was going to have to drive through Oregon before he turned north into Washington at Portland. There were mountains in northeast Oregon that they had to navigate, and they would have to drive through the Cascade Mountains along the Columbia River before they got to Portland.

Gladys was still white-knuckled going through the mountains. There were areas where there was no guardrail on the side of the road, and it was a sheer drop down on the passenger side. Peter thought it was fun driving these roads, but Gladys was terrified and let George know it. Twice, she had screamed very loudly. The road was narrow. They were lucky that they did not see another car coming toward them. George wasn't sure there was room for two vehicles side by side on the road, and with no shoulder, they would be in trouble.

Fortunately, they were able to get through the pass between La Grande and Pendleton, Oregon. The mountains were very high, and then they drove down into flat wheat fields closer to Pendleton.

George marveled at the way the fields looked. They were beautiful. He had not seen anything growing like that for several years. That was the way the fields looked in Missouri when they could produce a crop. There was water here for irrigation and men to work the fields.

George asked the owner of the filling station in Pendleton about the drive to Portland. The owner said that it could take as much as three days depending on the weather along the river. From The Dalles to Portland was in the Cascade Mountains, and the road was winding and rough in some places. The owner explained that the winter weather was on the mountain roads, and the repair crews took some time to get to all of them. He warned George to have his tires checked and to have a full tank of gas and a full spare tire before he left The Dalles.

Again, Gladys was scared to death of driving in the mountains. They were also told that they would be driving through some beautiful country and to enjoy it, but Gladys had her mind set that she was not going to admit to enjoying any part of the drive west. Even this far into the trip, she still kept saying she wanted to go home. At one point while they were going from La Grande to Pendleton, she begged George to turn around and take her home.

George was feeling the stress of her complaints but did not want to say anything in front of Peter. He would have to get to Raymond before they had any private time to talk. He just kept reminding her that they were going to make $100.00 a month, more money than they had seen in a very long time.

The drive along the Columbia River was indeed beautiful. George thought that the countryside looked a lot like the Missouri wheat fields of several years ago. The wheat was just sprouting out of the ground and, in a month, would be waving in the breeze.

As they drove along, they began to hear a roar coming from the river. Then they saw a waterfall in the middle of the river, with hundreds of Indians out on scaffolds built just in front of the falls. The Indians were standing on the scaffolds, spearing large fish just before they jumped the falls. They were getting hundreds of very large fish.

George pulled over to the side of the road, and he and Peter got out of the car to watch the activity both on the scaffolds and on the riverbank. The men were spearing the fish and putting them into woven baskets, then passing them to the women along the banks. They were cleaning the fish and preparing them to hang in the drying sheds. George thought it was a beautiful sight, and Peter was jumping up and down with excitement at seeing such a scene. Gladys was yelling at them to get back into the car. She thought it was too dangerous to be out there with all of those "savages." She just could not believe that the Indians were peaceful people now. She was absolutely convinced that they would hurt them in some way.

George and Peter pretty much ignored her and continued to watch the proceedings on the river. He knew that they were wasting precious time but didn't care at this point. He didn't know if Peter would ever have a chance to see anything like this again.

After a few more minutes, they got back into the car and drove on to The Dalles, Oregon. George found an inexpensive hotel for the night. There was a café off the lobby where they were able to have supper. The food was very good and plentiful for a little amount of money. The waitress told George that there was a lot of work being done along the river, and the workers came into the café for meals. They had to provide them with hearty meals for a little amount of money. They were doing a booming business.

They had a good night's sleep, and George and Peter were up early and ready for breakfast and to get on the road. George was anxious to get to his brother's house and stop driving.

Gladys was being stubborn and did not want to get out of bed, did not want to eat breakfast, and did not want to get back into the car and drive on. She was mumbling to herself that if she stalled, George might change his mind and turn around and go home.

"Peter and I are going into the diner to have breakfast. Then we are coming back to get our things, pack up the car, and go to the filling station to make sure that we are all set for the rest of the trip. If you are not ready by the time we get back, Peter and I will leave without you. We have about two or possibly three more days of travel before we get there. If you do not want to be left here by yourself, you will be ready when we get back from breakfast," George exclaimed.

When George and Peter sat down to eat, Peter asked his dad with a wide-eyed look on his face, "Would you really leave Mom here, Dad?"

"Right now, I don't know, Peter. Maybe for a few minutes. She is being irrational and not thinking straight," George explained. "No, I would not ever leave her for long. I love your mom too much to do that. But I want her to understand that we are not going back to Missouri. There is nothing left for us back there. Our future is out here. Your future is out here."

"Okay, Dad. Thanks for not thinking about leaving her by herself. I know she is really scared, but I am really excited about our new life here," Peter said.

"I am very glad you are, son," George answered.

"You know, Dad, Mom is not only afraid of the Indians and the mountain roads and the river, but she is afraid of Aunt Emma and Uncle Dan. She is afraid they won't like her," Peter explained.

"Why in the world would she be afraid of Dan and Emma? She doesn't even know them," George asked.

"I don't know, Dad. She just said she was," Peter answered.

George was very proud of Peter for speaking up and explaining some of Gladys' fears and concerns. He would try to be more tolerant of her from now on.

CHAPTER 5

When they got back to their room, Gladys was dressed and ready to go. George supposed that the fear of being left behind was greater than all of her other fears.

At the filling station, George made sure that all of the tires had air in them, including the spare tire. He checked the two canvas bags of water tied to the front of the car and made sure that the gas can was full. He also purchased an additional can of oil. They were ready to start the final days of their journey west.

As they drove along, George explained that the land they saw across the river was Washington. The river was the dividing line between the two states and flowed into the Pacific Ocean. He noticed a lot of little boats in the river with people fishing for salmon. They were not spearing them but using fishing poles to catch them.

George also told Peter how the salmon were migrating back to the area where they were born to lay their eggs. Sometimes they would swim hundreds of miles to get to the special place where they could lay their eggs. He was trying to explain to Peter what instinct was and how the salmon knew by instinct where to go.

"I know about instinct," announced Gladys. "My instinct tells me to go back home. This trip is a folly. I don't believe that your brother will pay you $100.00 a month to run a filling station. No one has that much money. When we get to his house, I want us to get on a train and go back to Missouri. We can find someplace to live, and you can find some work."

"We are not going back to Missouri," stated George. "Please get that idea out of your head, my dear. We are starting a new life here, and this is where we will stay. Please, let's not hear any more on that subject. I want to enjoy this beautiful scenery."

They had passed Hood River, Oregon, and were coming up on the new Bonneville Dam. The dam was finished in 1938 and was a sight to behold. George pulled off the road and drove into a parking lot. He and Peter got out of the car and walked to the lookout so they could see the dam. Both of them were fascinated and read a plaque that told about the building of the dam. Gladys was still mad and would not get out of the car.

After leaving the parking lot, they drove west and encountered some beautiful waterfalls along the highway. The tallest waterfall was called Multnomah Falls. There was a beautiful lodge with a restaurant there. George decided to treat them all to lunch in the restaurant. They had been very frugal with their money and deserved a nice lunch. After lunch, Peter ran up a trail toward the falls, and George and Gladys sat on a bench below the falls. It was truly a beautiful sight, and Gladys was even impressed by it, although she was still afraid of seeing the force of that much water in one place. She had never seen a waterfall before.

After leaving Multnomah Falls, they drove along a very winding road and encountered five more waterfalls, not as big as the first one, but still very impressive.

As they were rounding another curve in the road, they came upon a funny-looking building. It was an eight-sided building and was a rest stop for travelers along the Columbia River Highway. Again, Gladys was afraid of the height and would not get out of the car, but George and Peter enjoyed the view.

They had had a long day of driving with several more stops than they usually had. George was tired and wanted to find someplace to stay as soon as possible. It had started to rain earlier in the afternoon, and the skies didn't look like they were going to stop anytime soon. The idea of sleeping in the car was not a pleasant one.

They drove into the small town of Corbett, found a small hotel, and even though it was a little more than George wanted to spend for a room, he went ahead and took it. He was tired and needed a good night's sleep.

He talked to the desk clerk the next morning about driving through Portland and getting across the river into Washington. He was instructed to follow Highway 30 all the way into Portland until they reached Highway 99. They would turn right onto Highway 99 and head north across the bridge to Vancouver, Washington. From there, they would head north on Highway 99 to a town called Chehalis and then head west to Raymond. They should be there before 5:00 PM.

Gladys was getting more and more agitated as they got closer to their destination. They had followed the directions the desk clerk at the hotel had given them and had no trouble getting through Portland. Gladys was very scared driving across the bridge over the Columbia River. She was certain they would fall into the water. She was screaming most of the way across, and George had a hard time keeping her away from the steering wheel. She wanted to grab it or grab at his arm. As soon as he found a safe place to pull off the road, he pulled over and tried to calm her down.

"Gladys, you are going to have to calm down. You are scaring Peter, and you are going to cause us to have an accident if you don't stop," George insisted. "If you continue with your current behavior, I will have to tie your hands together. I don't want to have to do that, so please calm down and stay quiet for a while. It will not be long, and we will be at Dan and Emma's. Please, Gladys," George begged.

Gladys calmed down. The idea of having her hands tied together scared her even more, so she just shut her mouth and didn't say anything at all.

At noon, they came to a town called Longview, where they stopped and had some lunch. From there, they continued north on Highway 99 until they reached Chehalis. George stopped at the filling station to get fuel and check the radiator and the oil. It was raining fairly hard, and the wipers on the windshield were working hard. George had checked and rechecked the tarp over the top of the car to make sure it was tied securely. He did not want the wind to blow it off.

Again, George checked with the manager of the station about the directions to Raymond. The manager said the road was fairly good. It was bumpy, and they were working on part of it, so there might be some delays, but they should make it to Raymond by about 5:00 in the evening. George thanked him for the information and drove west, heading for Dan and Emma's and their final destination. He was anxious to see his brother again and to be able to get out of the car and not have to drive for a while.

Gladys had become just the opposite of what she was earlier. She had stopped talking. She gave quiet, mumbled responses to questions from both George and Peter, but otherwise seemed to just shut down. George was baffled by her actions. He figured she would open up when they arrived at Dan's house and she had Emma to talk to. She probably missed female companionship and conversation.

They pulled into Raymond about 5:15 in the evening and easily found the Texaco filling station with the sign that read, "Daniel Taylor, Proprietor," over the door.

George pulled up to one of the pumps, got out of the car, and saw his brother Dan come out of the door. Dan just stopped and looked at George, then walked over to him, shook his hand, and pulled him into an embrace.

"Boy, is it good to see you," Dan said. "You look tired, but good. How was the trip?" he asked.

"Long, exciting, nerve-wracking in places, beautiful. We are glad to finally be here," George answered.

Peter bounded out of the car then and ran around to greet his Uncle Dan.

"Hi! I'm Peter," he introduced himself.

"You can't be Peter. Peter is just a little baby. You are too old to be Peter," Dan teased.

"I grew up," Peter stated proudly.

"Well, Peter, it is good to meet the older Peter. Welcome to Raymond, Washington," Dan said as he gave Peter a hug.

"Gladys, why don't you get out of the car and greet Dan?" George asked his wife.

"I will just have to get back in when we drive on," Gladys exclaimed. "I will get out when we stop for the night."

George turned around so his voice wouldn't carry to Gladys and said to Dan, "She is having some readjustment problems. We have had a hard time all the way across the country," George said with an exasperated tone in his voice.

"Well, let's drive up to the house. Emma is excited to see you, and she has been cooking all day, so there is a feast for dinner tonight," Dan announced.

Dan and Emma had a very pretty house situated on a bluff overlooking the town of Raymond. There was only one house near them, and it was a large old Victorian house across the road.

Dan directed George to park his car in the garage. "You can park it in here until you get it unloaded so the rain doesn't damage anything. We do have room in the back of the garage for everything that you have brought with you. Then it can be parked at the side of the driveway. Emma does like to have her car in the garage so that she does not get wet when she gets into it."

Emma Taylor greeted the family at the front door. She was very formal in her greetings. She had never met Gladys or Peter and had only seen George once before, so this was all very new to her, too.

"Please come in. You all must be very tired of riding in a car," Emma commented. "Dinner will be ready in about a half hour. Gladys, if you would like to freshen up, the bathroom is at the end of the hallway."

There was a very quiet "thank you" that came from Gladys as she walked down the hall to the bathroom. Gladys had never seen a bathroom like this. It had a toilet, sink, and a bathtub all in one room. There were pretty towels hanging from bars on the wall and a couple of rugs on the floor. There was also a mirror above the sink. She grew up with an outhouse in the back of the house and had never had a bathtub as big as this one.

She turned the water on in the sink and noticed that one of the faucets poured out hot water and the other one cold. Oh, it would be so nice to sink down into that bathtub full of hot water. Maybe someday she would be able to do that.

Gladys went back to the living room and found everyone getting up to head into the dining room to eat. Dan and Emma had a separate room with a large table and matching chairs. There was a beautiful sideboard that matched the table and a tall glass display case filled with beautiful glass dishes and knick-knacks. The table had a beautiful cloth on it and very fine china dishes to eat off of. Gladys just hoped that Peter would be very careful.

There was so much food on the table. Neither Gladys, George, or Peter had seen that much food served for one meal in a long, long time.

As they were walking into the dining room, Gladys took Peter aside and warned him about being careful with the dishes and not to take more food than he thought he could eat.

"Okay, Mom! Dad already warned me to mind my manners," Peter told her.

Dan and George were busy talking about the filling station and what George's job would be, and Emma was talking to Peter about school. Peter told her that he was ready to go back to school and was excited about making new friends.

Emma tried a couple of times to include Gladys in the conversation, but Gladys would only give short, mumbled answers to her questions and did not add any additional content to the conversation.

When the meal was over, Emma got up to clear the table, and Gladys got up to help. "Oh, no! I will clear the table and wash the dishes. I would feel very bad if one of my dishes were broken," Emma said.

Gladys was stunned when Emma said that. "I would not break one of your dishes on purpose," Gladys said to her with an astonished look on her face. She was insulted by the comment.

"Oh, I know you wouldn't do it on purpose, but I will feel much better dealing with the cleaning up myself," Emma said in return.

From those comments, Gladys knew what her life was going to be like living here. This was not her home, and she would probably be asked to do the menial work. Gladys wondered if George knew what Emma was really like. The problem was, he would be upset with her if she tried to tell him. He would say she was continuing the same complaint.

Gladys was well aware that she was not raised with the same advantages as Emma and that she did not have all of the nice things that Emma had, but she was raised by parents who loved her and taught her proper manners and the value of friendship and love. She was raised according to the Golden Rule, and she had always tried to live by it.

George, Gladys, and Peter all had bedrooms in the basement. It was a beautifully finished basement with their own bathroom. Peter was very excited to have a room of his own. On the farm, he had slept on a pallet in the corner of the living room. There was only one bedroom in the house.

George had decided that it was necessary for Peter to start school right away. Dan explained that there were only two weeks left before summer break, but George was adamant. He wanted Peter to have the opportunity to meet some boys in his class and possibly make some friends. Peter was all for starting school now. He wanted to make some friends. It would make the summer a lot more fun if he had some guys to hang around with. He was getting tired of being around the adults all the time. Anyway, Peter liked school. He liked learning new things.

Gladys, on the other hand, wasn't sure she wanted Peter that far away from her all day. She was very nervous about having him around strangers. There were so many chances that he could get hurt or into trouble. George assured her that he would be fine, that the school was close, and if anything happened to him, they would be able to get there fast.

George, Gladys, and Dan all took Peter to school on Monday. The principal decided that Peter would be put into the fourth grade. He was a very bright boy and was reading far above his grade level. They were all introduced to Miss Virginia Prine, the fourth and fifth-grade teacher. Dan already knew Miss Prine; she was a customer of his at the filling station. Peter liked her immediately. She shook his hand and treated him like an adult. She did not ignore him or talk down to him. He felt important. But, again, Gladys was hesitant to leave him there. She wanted to delay his starting school until September, but George vetoed her.

CHAPTER 6

When Peter was all set at his new school, Dan took George and Gladys back home. There was a whole lot of paperwork that needed to be done, especially when the station was busy. It would take some time to get used to this kind of work. He had been a farmer for his entire life and knew no other profession.

George and Dan went home at lunchtime for George to get his car. Dan had to spend the afternoon at the distribution office, so George was on his own except for the young boy who worked part-time for Dan.

Emma was not there when they got home. Gladys was down in the basement in their bedroom, just sitting on a chair, doing nothing.

When George asked her why she was down here all alone, she said, "Because Emma told me not to worry about anything. She had supper all planned. So, I came down here so I wouldn't disturb anything."

"I'm sure Emma didn't mean you have to hide down here," George responded.

"I'm not so sure, George," Gladys said. "Every time I would look at something upstairs and ask about it, she would tell me to be very careful with it. It was either an antique or very precious to her. She treats me like I'm a little child about ready to break all of her fine china. I might not have been raised with fancy things, but I am not a total screw-up," Gladys cried.

"I know, dear. We will work out the problem. I will talk to Dan and see if we can come to some terms as to the division of the chores. Did Emma say where she was going?" asked George.

"She had some sort of committee meeting to go to for one of the organizations she belongs to. She really didn't explain, just left and told me not to worry about dinner; she had it all taken care of," Gladys responded.

"I need to get some lunch and get back to the station. It was fairly busy this morning. I think I am going to enjoy this job. I will meet a lot of the people in town," George explained.

"I'm glad you will enjoy it," she said very sadly.

"Let's find the local Baptist church and go on Sunday morning. Maybe you will be able to meet some ladies there," George suggested.

On Sunday morning, Emma and Dan, George and Gladys, and Peter piled into Dan's car and went off to the Redeemer Baptist Church. Both Emma and Dan were active in the church activities and were happy to introduce George, Gladys, and Peter to the congregation.

The Baptist church that George and Gladys went to in Memphis, Missouri, had a very active youth group, a women's prayer group, and a sewing group. The men met once a week for prayer and discussions of the Bible. The preacher gave a very emotional and fiery sermon every Sunday.

They sat in the church in Raymond and were stunned at how quiet it was. The congregation only sang one hymn, and the choir tried to sing an anthem but were off-key. The pianist hit more wrong keys than right ones, and the preacher talked in a monotone. George almost went to sleep, and Peter sat in the pew between his parents, squirming and swinging his legs back and forth. He was thoroughly bored.

When the service was over, they expected a coffee time afterward, but all they did was walk out the door, shake hands with the preacher, who didn't even ask for their names, and got in the car to drive home.

"That was a very quiet service for a Baptist church," Gladys mentioned. "I expected a little more enthusiasm in the singing."

Emma responded in a sedate manner, "We do not care for the 'hellfire and brimstone' way of preaching here. We prefer a more sedate service."

"I can see that," George said rather sarcastically.

Emma had planned a very formal Sunday dinner to be eaten at 3:00 PM. "On Sundays, we prefer our meal in the afternoon." When Gladys offered to help, Emma refused, saying that she had everything under control and preferred to fix meals by herself.

The meal was very good, but again when Gladys offered to help with the cleanup, the answer was "No." So, she went down to their bedroom, laid down on the bed, and went to sleep.

When Gladys awoke, it was nighttime, and George was in bed beside her.

"I am sorry, George, but I cannot stand living here. There is nothing for me to do. She won't let me touch her precious dishes or help cook anything. I can't even help with the cleanup. She has a special way of doing everything, and she says my help in the kitchen would make it too hard for her," Gladys complained.

"I know, dear," George answered. "I am going to talk to Dan about it and see if there is an apartment or house in town that we can rent at a reasonable rate. We have very little money left, and we might have to wait for my first paycheck, but we will find a place as soon as we can. I do not want Peter growing up with the attitude they have. Unfortunately, Dan is becoming the same self-centered person that his wife is. He is letting me handle the filling station, but with a long rope attached."

"Do you suppose there is another Baptist church in the area?" Gladys asked.

"I don't know, but South Bend is just up the road ways, and they might have one. We can certainly take a drive up there and check it out. Anything is better than what we heard this morning. I almost went to sleep, and Peter was bouncing around like a rubber ball," George commented.

Monday was a busy day at the filling station. George and Carl, the part-time worker, were busy all day, so George did not have time to talk to Dan about Emma and Gladys. He was really concerned about Gladys and her state of mind. Dinner Monday evening was the same as before. Gladys was not allowed to help with the preparations or the cleanup.

"George, would you take a walk with me? I need to work off some of this frustration before I say something I will regret," Gladys whispered to George.

"Sure. Do you want your sweater?" George asked as he headed to their bedroom to get their sweaters. It got cool in the early evening hours, and the wind was coming up.

They walked a few blocks before Gladys said anything. "Something's got to change, George, or else I will get on a train and go back to Missouri. I don't know where I will get the money, but I will find it somewhere. We have been here for two weeks, and I have not been allowed to do anything. For God's sake, I am not two years old. She lets Peter do things with her in the kitchen that I am not allowed to do," cried Gladys.

"I know, dear. It was so busy today that I didn't have a chance to talk to Dan, but I will make the time tomorrow, I promise," George assured her.

They turned around and slowly walked back to the house. Gladys felt better just being able to hold George's hand while they walked. Public affection was frowned upon in Dan and Emma's house. Gladys wanted to be away from Emma and all of her 'things' and her ideas.

Tuesday dawned rainy, wet, and cold—a truly miserable Northwest day outside. Fortunately, there was a cover over the gas pumps at the station, so George didn't get the full impact of the downpour, but the wind whipped the cold rain on him anyway. Dan stopped by the station at noon with a couple of sandwiches and a thermos of hot coffee. As yesterday was so busy, today was slow. There had been only four cars in all morning to fill up and two cars in for minor emergency repairs. A couple of vehicles pulled in for directions to the beach, although why anyone would want to go to the beach on a day like today was beyond George's imagination.

"George, I need to get right to the point. Emma is very nervous about Gladys wanting to help around the house. She is very possessive about her things and doesn't want anyone else touching them. Could you please ask Gladys not to offer to help?" Dan asked.

"And just what is she supposed to do, Dan? She is new to the area and doesn't know anyone yet. You did not introduce us to anyone except the pastor on Sunday at church. I know neither one of us is sophisticated, but we are decent people with a desire to help where we can," George explained. "Gladys is ready to get on a train and go back to Missouri. If she goes, Peter and I go too. There is nothing for us back there, but we will find something somehow. Life is too short to be miserable and unappreciated."

"I will talk to Emma," Dan said. "In the meantime, I will start looking for an apartment for you to rent. Maybe it will be better if you, Gladys, and Peter have your own place. There are a few apartment buildings in town, and the rents are reasonable."

"But, Daniel," Emma said, "she has never handled fine china before. She is from a farm in rural Missouri. How could she know what to do or how to set a table properly?"

"Stop! You are talking about my brother's wife. She is not a hick from the hills of West Virginia. She is a lady and deserves our respect. Just because they have not had the monetary advantages that we have had doesn't mean that they are any less of a person. And they are my family! I think you owe her an apology, Emma," Dan scolded. "You treat Peter better than you treat his mother."

"Peter is a very well-mannered young man," stated Emma.

"And where have you seen evidence of bad manners from Gladys? You haven't because she is a very well-mannered lady. Anyway, I am going to start looking for a place for them to stay. They need their own place where Gladys can feel like she is needed and has something to do, even if it is fixing a meal and cleaning up after her family," Daniel said.

Emma stiffened her back, pinched her lips together, and said, "Maybe that would be for the best."

Dan turned and walked out of the kitchen, very upset with his wife's attitude toward his brother and sister-in-law.

Two days later, Dan stopped by the filling station on his way to a meeting to see George. "I think I have found the perfect solution to your problem, George. There is a lady in town who lives in a beautiful home but cannot take care of it anymore. She is the widow of one of the founders of the sawmill. She needs some live-in help. She cannot be by herself any longer. Her granddaughter is living with her now, but she wants to go away to school and cannot leave until her grandmother is taken care of."

"You would be living in her house and have full use of it. There would be a small salary for Gladys, as she would be the primary caregiver. You would continue to work here but maybe do some of the repair work that needs to be done around her house. What do you think?" Dan asked.

"I think it sounds perfect," George answered. "When can we meet her? I'm sure she wants to meet us and check us out before inviting us to live in her home with her."

"How about tonight?" Dan asked.

"Perfect! I will tell Gladys and Peter to be ready."

"By the way, her name is Gertrude Carpenter, but she hates to be called Gertrude. She is Trudy!" Dan explained.

"I will pass that on. Thanks, Dan. You are a good brother," George said as he shook Dan's hand.

George explained the situation to Gladys as soon as he got home. For the first time since they arrived in Raymond, she had a hopeful look on her face. And Peter was just as excited when he heard the news.

CHAPTER 7

Trudy Carpenter was a small lady with a big smile and laugh lines all over her very sweet face. She was crippled up with arthritis and in a wheelchair most of the time. She was able to move herself onto her sofa in the living room but had a hard time getting back into her chair. She needed twenty-four-hour care.

Her home was large and airy, but her husband had been dead for over 20 years, so much of the maintenance on the place had not been done. The plumbing needed some repair, and several of the boards on the main floor needed to be nailed down. Both the interior and exterior of the house needed painting, and it needed a general scrubbing down.

George, Gladys, and Peter made a very good impression on Trudy, and she hired them that evening. Gladys explained that she cooked good, nutritious food and did not do anything fancy. She loved to bake and made all of her own bread back on the farm. Trudy was thrilled with the idea of homemade bread. She hadn't had it since she was able to bake it herself.

"My granddaughter will be here until Saturday when she is going into Tacoma to school at Pacific Lutheran College. She wants to become a nurse but also wants to take some of the basic courses she needs to get a bachelor's degree before she goes to nursing school. She is very ambitious and a very good student. I am very proud of her," Trudy explained.

"What is a bachelor's degree?" asked Peter with a curious look on his face.

"That is a degree you get when you graduate from college," Trudy explained.

Peter looked up at his parents and said, "I think I will get one of those someday." They all laughed at the matter-of-fact way he said it, but all agreed that it was a grand ambition.

"How about moving in on Saturday? I will have Sally go to the grocery store and pick up a few things for our dinner. Do you make meatloaf, Gladys? I love meatloaf and mashed potatoes with gravy," Trudy said.

"Mom makes a great meatloaf. It is one of my favorites, especially when she puts all of that good brown gravy on top," chimed in Peter.

Trudy laughed and said that it would be meatloaf for dinner Sunday. She was going to love having Peter around.

"Do you like cherry pie, Mrs. Carpenter? I could make a cherry pie for dessert. It would top off the meatloaf meal very nicely," Trudy asked.

"First of all, please call me Trudy, and yes, I do love cherry pie. I love any kind of pie. I will have Sally pick up some cherries and the rest of the supplies you need for making a pie. Please, before you leave today, check out the pantry and make a list of what supplies you will need. Sally will pick them up for you."

Friday's evening meal at Dan and Emma's was stiff and very formal, with not much conversation between the adults. Peter was as talkative as ever but was quieted by the fact that the adults were not responding to him as they usually did. Emma was not happy with Dan for recommending George and Gladys to Trudy Carpenter. Dan had explained to her that Trudy needed the help, and Emma, in turn, stated that Trudy Carpenter was a much more sophisticated woman and Gladys just wasn't the type of person to tend to her needs. Emma knew that Gladys didn't have the level of sophistication that Trudy needed.

"Trudy seems very happy with them taking care of her and the house. George is a very good carpenter, and in his spare time, he will work on some of the repairs that are needed," Dan explained. "Please, Emma, give Gladys a chance. All she and George want is a chance to make a good life here. They have been through some rough times and deserve to have some peace and happiness for a change. They had no chance at all of getting ahead back in the Midwest. We certainly have been affected by the Depression here, but not anything like they were in the Midwest. Here, they have a chance of getting ahead, and Trudy Carpenter is giving them that chance."

"It seems to me that you started it all by sending them all that money," Emma countered. "You know that I did not approve of that."

"I need the help at the station, Emma. I can't run the distribution center and the filling station at the same time. I need someone I can trust, and I trust George. Now, let's drop it. What's done is done," Dan said.

George, Gladys, and Peter moved into Trudy Carpenter's home on Saturday. Dan had a truck that they loaded up with all of their things and were able to move everything in one trip. Trudy let them store the things that they would not need in her garage. There was still room for George's car in there, too.

Gladys asked for permission to change some things around in the kitchen. Gladys was left-handed, and the kitchen was set up backwards for her.

"You go ahead and change whatever you want. I am not able to work in there anymore and rarely enter the room. So, it is your territory now. Please let me know if there is anything you need," Trudy told her.

"I will admit, I have never cooked on an electric stove before. I had a wood stove on the farm, and that is all I have ever used. I noticed that you have a manual for the stove in one of the drawers. I will be reading it carefully in the next few days. I hope that I don't ruin the meatloaf tomorrow evening," Gladys said.

"I have every confidence in you, my dear," Trudy said as she slowly wheeled herself into her bedroom. She was able to get herself on and off of her bed from her chair, but Gladys followed her to make sure she was okay.

The next week was a busy one for both George and Gladys. George was driving back and forth to work at the filling station, and Gladys was thriving in her new job as caregiver to Trudy Carpenter. As Trudy predicted, the meatloaf that Gladys fixed was perfect, and she had made enough for sandwiches the next day.

Usually in the evening after dinner, Trudy, George, and Gladys sat in the living room and listened to the news on the radio. One of their favorite newscasters was Edward R. Murrow. He would broadcast a show every evening from London, England. He was very frank and graphic in his broadcasting, and the listeners felt that they were hearing the truth from him. Unfortunately, the news was not good. England was being bombed by the Germans, and they were suffering greatly. It seemed that Hitler and the Nazis were conquering all of Europe. So far, the United States had been able to stay out of the conflict but were sending aid to the British, who were taking a real pounding from the German bombs. The news wasn't any better from the Pacific side of the United States. The Japanese were intent on taking as much territory as they could. People who lived on the Pacific Coast were worried about the Japanese invading the United States, but it was a long way from Japan to Washington State.

Peter was loving his new school. He was a good student and a good athlete. He loved to play basketball. Trudy let George put a hoop up on the front of the garage so Peter and his friends could practice. He would come home, do his homework, and go out and shoot hoops. Several of his friends would come over, and they would have impromptu games. Trudy loved to listen to the boys chattering as they were playing. Gladys was afraid that the boys would be too noisy, but Trudy loved having them there. She felt it brought life back into her days.

The holidays were quiet and subdued at the Taylor/Carpenter residence. Emma and Dan had Gladys, George, and Peter over for dinner, and Trudy Carpenter went to be with her daughter, son-in-law, and granddaughter in South Bend for the day. The war was raging in Europe, and the United States government was in talks with the Japanese over China and Southeast Asia. The year 1941 promised to be more of the same, and the outlook was not real positive for any improvement. President Roosevelt had kept us out of the fighting, but no one knew for how long that would last.

In October 1941, George got a call from Dan at the distribution center asking him to come to his office. There was a young man working part-time at the filling station, so George was able to get away. He walked the three blocks down the road to Dan's office and walked directly in to see Dan.

"What's up?" George asked.

"I have just received a message from the United States Army asking me about fuel reserves and how much I can stockpile here. I perceive that to mean that gasoline is going to be rationed soon and most of the supply will be going to the army. That will also mean that the supply for the general public to purchase will be rationed, which means that the filling station will not have a lot of extra fuel to sell. I don't know whether I will be able to keep you on full-time or not," Dan explained to George. "I think you should go to the lumber mill and see what sorts of jobs are available there. The military is going to need lumber, and the mills will be ramping up production and will need additional help. Trudy might be able to give you a name of someone to talk to," Dan suggested. George sat in the chair across from Dan with his chin down on his chest. The thought of being unemployed again was very scary to him.

"Thanks for the heads up, Dan. How long do you think it will be before the changes are made?" George asked.

"I don't know, but from the headlines and news broadcasts, I wouldn't think it would be long. Maybe a couple of months," Dan speculated.

That evening, George explained the situation to both Gladys and Peter. He wanted Peter to be aware of what was going on and the changes that would be made to their lives.

The next morning, George stayed at home later so that he could talk to Trudy. She agreed that the lumber mill would probably be the only business in town that would be ramping up their number of employees. She also mentioned that if they did have the misfortune of getting into this war, many of the young men would be leaving, and they would certainly need the extra help. While George was still there, she called Phillip Waring, the personnel manager at Carpenter Lumber, gave him George's name, and let him know that George would be in to see what was available in full-time work.

Phil was always glad to get a referral from Trudy Carpenter. He could always count on her to give him good leads for new employees. He let Trudy know that he would be available about 4:30, and if George wanted to come in then, he would be glad to talk to him.

George called Dan and let him know what was going on and that he would be taking the entire day off. Gladys wanted to do some shopping, and there were some repairs that George needed to do on Trudy's house that would become critical if not done soon. He also told him that he had an appointment with the personnel manager at the lumber mill that afternoon.

"George, I hate to lose you as an employee, but I know that this will be the best move for you. Thanks for calling, and I will see you tomorrow. Good luck this afternoon," Dan said as he hung up the phone.

George arrived right on time for his appointment with Phillip Waring. Phil gave George a tour of the mill, showing him every facet of the operation, from the time the logs came from the woods to when they were loaded onto trains as either raw boards or finished lumber. Some of the trains were headed for the docks at Tacoma and Seattle, some south to San Francisco and beyond, and some of them were headed east to cities in the Midwest.

George was fascinated with the whole process. He had never seen logs that big before. Missouri did not have a lot of timberland and certainly not the large fir and pine trees that the Northwest had. George was most interested in the large band saws that cut the huge logs into boards. He watched the crew change one of the dull blades for a sharp one and watched the process of moving that huge blade to the sharpening area, where a man was busy getting the blade ready for use again.

Phil explained to George that they always had a blade that was sharp and ready to put back onto the saw. During the peak times, it was not cost-effective to have any downtime on the saw. They were currently working a day and a swing shift, and if the country entered the war, they would probably add a graveyard shift also.

"I would have thought that you sent them out to be sharpened," George commented.

"No, that would be too cost prohibitive. We do it right on site. It is much easier and keeps our expenses down, even though we are paying someone to sharpen them," Phil answered. "Are you interested in learning how to sharpen one of those blades?" Phil asked.

"Yes, I am!" answered George. "It looks like something that I would enjoy doing. It uses a skill and expertise that, unfortunately, a lot of jobs do not offer right now."

"It so happens that in about a month, we will be looking for a new saw filer. Len over here is going to retire after about 25 years of working in the lumber industry, and a lot of the young men in the mill will probably be leaving for the military if we get into the war, which I suspect we will," Phil explained.

"Let's go into the office and fill out some forms. I will need to run a security check on you. Because we are sending lumber to the Army, they require that all of our employees have a security check, but that is a simple process. I will also need to see your driver's license and draft card," Phil said.

"I have them both with me," answered George.

CHAPTER 8

George worked at the filling station until the clearance came through for him to start work at the lumber mill. He was excited about the chance to learn a new trade.

Gladys was enjoying cooking for Trudy. She was getting used to using the electric stove and hadn't burned too many dinners. Trudy loved her healthy meals and seemed to feel better now that she was eating better. Even the dusting, vacuuming, and scrubbing of floors was more enjoyable for Gladys. Their house on the farm in Missouri was always dusty. There was dust here, but nothing like what she had on the farm.

Peter was on summer break from school and was having fun playing basketball with his friends. Trudy was always happy to have the boys at the house and said that it brought life back into the place.

George, Gladys, and Peter didn't see a lot of Dan and Emma. Everyone was busy with their own lives. George missed his brother but knew that it was tense every time Gladys and Emma got together. Emma was not at all happy that Gladys was the caregiver for Trudy Carpenter and actually living in her house. She was upset with Dan for recommending her for the job. As far as Emma was concerned, Gladys was not of the same social caliber as Trudy and was not fit to tend to her needs or take care of her property in her home.

One Sunday morning, when Emma knew that George, Gladys, and Peter were in church in South Bend, she paid Trudy a visit.

"I haven't been to see you in quite a while, and I knew that my brother-in-law and his family would be in church, so I thought I would drop in. How are you doing, Trudy? It must really be a trial having someone as unsophisticated as Gladys Taylor living in your home and supposedly taking care of you. I am surprised you have lasted as long as you have with her here," Emma expounded.

"I am not sure what you are talking about. I love having Gladys Taylor as my caregiver. All three of the Taylors are delightful, and I count them as some of my dearest friends. You have become a real snob, Emma. I am surprised at you. Gladys Taylor is part of your family, and you should embrace her and make friends with her. She is a wonderful lady!" Trudy announced.

"Well, I don't see it that way. She is a hick from Eastern Missouri, grew up on a poor dirt farm, and has had no education to speak of. She is like a mouse," Emma stated emphatically.

"Emma, if you cannot say anything nice about someone, keep your mouth closed. I would ask you to leave now. Your manners are worse than those of a hick from a dirt farm in Eastern Missouri," Trudy declared.

Emma rose from the chair with a huff and marched out of the house. Trudy was laughing when Emma slammed the door.

Because George spent a lot of his weekend time doing repairs and general maintenance on Trudy's house, Peter had taken over the job of mowing the lawn. He was getting better at it all the time. The only time he didn't enjoy it was when his friends wanted to shoot hoops and he had to finish the mowing before he could join them.

All three Taylors loved the rain. It had been so long since they had any significant rain in Missouri. They had light drizzles, but a real downpour that did the land or crops any good had not occurred in several years. That was one of the reasons they had to leave the farm. The rain in Washington was so refreshing and clean.

George was up very early every morning to be at work at 6:00 AM when his shift started. Gladys got up with him to fix him a good breakfast and to pack him a lunch. He had mentioned that he would need to do some reading and studying in order to learn the ins and outs of sharpening the big saw blades, and he would have to put aside some of the repairs on the house. He would devote his weekends, except for church time, to the maintenance work.

"I have never had to work to learn a trade before, so all of this studying is foreign to me. Farming came naturally because I grew up with it. The same with working on the car and machinery. I grew up with it and had to keep the farm machinery in good working order, but this book studying to learn a trade is different," George explained to Gladys. "Thank goodness for Peter and his good study habits. He is teaching me how to study. He thinks it is fun to study together. I don't know about fun, but I am learning."

It was three months before George felt confident enough to sharpen a saw blade on his own. His supervisor, Jonathan Kramer, felt that George was very capable of handling one of the big blades by himself. And Jonathan pronounced the job well done when George had finished his first one. All he needed now was experience to increase his speed and get the blades done sooner.

The war in Europe was not going well for the British or the French, and the United States was still refusing to get into the conflict. Most everyone thought it was inevitable that the U.S. would join in the fighting, and the country, as a whole, was gearing up toward that end. There were still a faction of the population who were adamantly against becoming involved. Even the Carpenter Lumber Mill in Raymond, Washington, was headed in the direction of war. An increasing number of orders were coming in from the Army for lumber to be shipped to Fort Lewis for the building of additional housing units for soldiers. The mill had gone to three shifts a day, and they were all busy. There was very little downtime. When a saw blade needed to be sharpened, it was taken off, moved to the filer to be sharpened, and a spare blade put on immediately. There was always a sharp replacement blade available.

George was not eligible for the draft because of his age and the fact that he had asthma. Gladys was very thankful that Peter was too young. School had started in September of 1941, and Peter was having a great time. He was a good student, did his homework in a timely manner, and was out shooting hoops as often as possible. When the weather was good, sometimes the boys would go to the school play field and play baseball, but they much preferred basketball.

Trudy's health seemed to be declining, even though she was eating better now and getting the proper care at home. Age was catching up with her. She shared the same August birthday as Peter. Peter turned 11 years old, and Trudy turned 87. Gladys planned a combined birthday party for them, and Trudy reveled in the fact that all of those young boys were at her birthday party. Her daughter, son-in-law, and granddaughter all came to the party. Gladys had made it a special day for both of them.

Dan and Emma came for cake and ice cream, and Dan was talked into helping turn the crank on the ice cream maker. Emma was very subdued and quiet but polite to all who were in attendance. She knew she had made a fool of herself with Trudy earlier and wasn't about to do a repeat performance.

Dan and Emma had given Peter a bicycle for his birthday, and he was so excited. He had transportation! All of the boys took a turn riding it up and down the street in front of Trudy's house.

George and Gladys had found a church to attend in South Bend that was more to their liking. Emma was offended that they would not attend church with them, but George explained to her that they were not used to a quiet, subdued service like the Raymond church had. They wanted more singing and a livelier message, and the South Bend Baptist Church provided that for them. Trudy Carpenter used to attend the Baptist Church in South Bend and was excited about the Taylors attending there.

Since Trudy was not able to get out very often, she invited the ladies' Bible study group to come to her home every Wednesday afternoon, and they readily accepted. The ladies missed seeing Trudy, and Gladys was a welcome addition to the group.

Dan and Emma felt left out of George and Gladys' activities now. Emma realized that she pushed Gladys away but still wasn't willing to let her help with dinner or cleanup when they did come to dinner. She also still felt that Gladys wasn't good enough to take care of Trudy.

The holidays were fast approaching, and Gladys was preparing to fix a traditional Thanksgiving dinner for Trudy, her daughter, son-in-law, and granddaughter. Trudy had not been able to have her family at her home for a holiday meal for a long time, and she was enjoying the planning and preparations for the meal. Gladys was very good about including Trudy in every decision that was made. Trudy invited Dan and Emma, but they declined, saying they had been invited elsewhere. After the meal, the men retired to the living room to listen to the football game, and the women went to the kitchen for cleanup duty. Trudy went to her room to lay down for a while.

As Trudy's family was leaving with a healthy portion of the leftovers, her daughter thanked Gladys for taking such good care of her mother and for being such a good friend to her.

"George," Gladys said as they were getting ready for bed that evening, "I was so scared to come here, and I was so unhappy at Dan and Emma's, but I feel like I have a purpose now, and I am happy we are here. We have so many more opportunities here, and Peter has a bright future ahead of him. We do have a lot to be

thankful for this holiday season."

CHAPTER 9

On December 7, 1941, George, Gladys, and Peter were driving back from church in South Bend. They had enjoyed the service that morning as it was the beginning of the Christmas season and always a joyous time in the life of the church. Being able to sing the familiar Christmas carols and hear the story of the impending birth of the Christ Child was always a thrill, no matter how many times they had heard it.

The service lasted a little longer than usual, and Gladys was anxious to get back to Trudy. She had the beginnings of a cold, and Gladys was worried about her. She had said that she would stay home from church, but Trudy insisted she go with her family.

Trudy was no better when they got home, and Gladys wanted to call the doctor, but Trudy insisted that she would be okay. A cup of hot tea with honey in it would be the best remedy.

After lunch, George sat down in front of the radio to listen to a ball game when a news bulletin interrupted the game. The Japanese had bombed Pearl Harbor in the Hawaiian Islands. George called for Gladys to come and listen.

"We are in this war now for sure," George commented. "All the young men will be enlisting in the service. God help us!"

The next day, President Roosevelt declared war on Japan. Because of the proximity of Raymond to the Pacific Ocean, the city and area around it were put on high alert for possible attack by the Japanese.

Trudy Carpenter and the Taylor family knew that their whole way of life was going to change. The Carpenter Lumber Mill was already supplying lumber for defense housing on Fort Lewis and the Bremerton Ship Yard.

"Thank God Peter is too young to go into the military," whispered Gladys to Trudy. "Too many of the young men will be leaving. I am afraid this will be a grim Christmas season with so many going to war."

"I agree with you about a grim holiday. My daughter just called a bit ago to see how I was and said that my son-in-law will enlist as soon as he can. He is a trained firefighter and feels that he will be needed. I worry sick about him now when he has to go out on a job. I don't know what it will be like when he is gone. I guess I can't fault him for his desire to help, but it doesn't make me worry any less," Trudy commented.

"You know, I still would like George and Peter to get a Christmas tree for us to decorate. I have so many decorations up in the attic and would like to use them this year," Trudy added.

"I am sure that they would be glad to do that for you. Is there an area where they can cut down their own tree? Peter would be very excited about that," Gladys asked.

"Oh yes, I will give George the directions. I think I will lay down for a while. This has been a stressful day, and I have a feeling the days ahead will be just as or more upsetting," Trudy commented.

The tree was cut and brought into the house. The decorations were lovely. Trudy had some old, very fragile glass decorations, and then she had some that her daughter and granddaughter had made. The tree was festive and beautiful. Peter was entranced by the volume of decorations on the tree. He had never seen one quite like it before.

There were a few gifts exchanged on Christmas Day, but most of the day was spent in front of the radio listening to war news.

The United States had also declared war on Germany, so would be fighting on two fronts. That would mean more young men would be drafted, more young men would be leaving, and unfortunately, more young men would not be returning. It was a scary time for everyone.

George was busy all day. He would sometimes have to snatch his lunch in between working on saw blades. Production had increased since war was declared. All three shifts were working to capacity. Since more young men were leaving for the service, more facilities had to be built at the military bases. Lumber was being shipped by rail both to Fort Lewis and Bremerton, and it was also being sent by rail to California to the military bases down there. The rail cars were coming into the mill empty and leaving full of cut lumber. Every lumber mill in Oregon and Washington was running at capacity in order to fill the needs.

The school break for the Christmas holiday was rather bleak for the students this year. Peter's friends with older brothers were worried about them enlisting or being drafted and having to go to either Europe or to the Pacific. People were trying to be optimistic about 1942 and hoping for a quick end to both conflicts, but the forecasters predicted that it would be a long conflict before Germany and Japan would surrender.

Unfortunately, Trudy Carpenter's health was declining. She had a mild stroke in March 1942 and was unable to get in and out of her wheelchair by herself. She needed constant help. Her daughter came on Sundays to be with her so Gladys could have some time off. She was able to go to church with George and Peter and know that Trudy was taken care of. She would get home from church and fix a meal for all of them, but more often than not, Trudy was not able to join them. Gladys would take her a tray in her room.

"George, what will happen to us when Trudy is no longer here?" Gladys asked her husband one day at breakfast. Trudy had had a particularly hard night and needed Gladys's help several times in the middle of the night, and Gladys was extremely worried about her.

"I suppose we will have to find a place to live. I would imagine that her family would want to sell this place. I have not been able to complete all of the repairs because of work, so it still needs some work done on it before they could sell it."

By April 1942, Trudy was almost bedridden, and her daughter and son-in-law made the decision to place her in a nursing home. She needed round-the-clock nursing care, more than Gladys was capable of giving her.

The Parkers knew that they had to find a new place to live and were concerned, but Trudy's son-in-law asked if they would be willing to stay in the house and finish the repairs and the painting. The repairs and painting needed to be done before the house could be put up for sale. George and Gladys were very happy to stay and finish the work. George was working six days a week at the mill, but thought that he would be able to complete the work on the house in about three months.

"George, I will be able to do the inside painting," Gladys said. "Without Trudy to take care of, I have a lot of free time."

"Thanks, dear. You would be able to get a lot of the work done, and I would be able to do the repairs in the evenings and on Sundays. We can put Peter to work doing the necessary yard work. I know he doesn't like to do a lot of it, but sometimes we have to do things we don't particularly like, and there is no better time for him to learn that lesson than now. This will give us a reprieve on finding a new place to live," George added.

Trudy Carpenter passed away peacefully in May 1942. The town turned out in full force for her funeral service and burial. Gladys was bereft at her passing. Trudy was the first real friend she had made in Raymond. She had other friends from church, but Trudy was her first real confidant. She, George, and Peter were able to stay in the house until October when Trudy's family finally put the house up for sale. They were able to stay in the house until it sold, but all of Trudy's personal belongings and much of the furniture were removed. The kitchen equipment was left until the sale was complete. Most of Gladys's kitchen utensils were still in storage in Dan and Emma's garage but were moved over to Trudy's garage for storage until they found a place of their own.

During the first week of October, George and Gladys started looking for another place to live. They had never had to pay rent before, so the whole process of finding and applying for an apartment or house to rent was foreign to them.

They finally found an apartment in Raymond that they could afford and moved into it the third weekend of October. They had very little furniture but were able to go to the thrift store and purchase a bed for themselves and one for Peter. They also found a kitchen table and four chairs. With a little paint and some chair cushions, they would be just perfect for their small kitchen. Dan and Emma had an extra sofa and chair stored in their basement and loaned them to George and Gladys until they could get one of their own. They had brought their radio all the way from Missouri and were finally able to use it.

Gladys was happy to be able to use her own kitchen utensils again. They weren't as nice as the ones that Trudy had, but she was used to them, and they were her own.

Peter adjusted to his new surroundings very nicely. The only thing that he missed was the basketball hoop at Trudy's, but since he had a bicycle now, he was able to go to the schoolyard to shoot hoops with his friends, and with the radio set up, he was glad to be able to listen to "The Shadow" again. Trudy didn't really like the show, so it was never turned on.

The holiday season in 1942 was bleak. The fighting in both Europe and the South Pacific was not going well for the Allies, and the news headlines were grim.

In January 1943, Raymond reported its first casualty of the war. He was a young boy who had graduated from Raymond High School in 1941. He had enlisted in the Marine Corps right out of high school, anticipating that the United States would eventually get into the war. He was sent to Hawaii, then on to a remote island in the South Pacific. He was killed by enemy fire while storming another small island. His name was David Gillespie, and when his body was returned to his family, the whole town turned out for his funeral. It was a sad time for the town.

Gladys felt adrift after they moved from Trudy's house to the apartment. She had nothing to do. In decent weather, George was able to walk the few blocks to the mill, and Gladys was able to use the car, although they had to watch their gasoline consumption because of rationing. Most of the time, she would walk to the grocery store, which was only a few blocks away from home. She had a few friends in the ladies' Bible study group at the church in South Bend, but again, because of rationing, she hated to go that far just for an hour's Bible class and visit. She thought about getting a job, maybe some job that was left vacant by a man leaving for the war, but the lumber mill did not let women work in the actual mill, and they had plenty of office help. The Texaco distributorship owned by her brother-in-law Dan had plenty of help. There wasn't much of anything else available in town that she was qualified to do.

So, for something to do, Gladys pulled out her old sewing machine that they had brought from Missouri and started sewing. She would go to the thrift store and, for either 5 or 10 cents, buy dresses and remake them so they looked like new. Then she would sell them for 25 or 50 cents. The ladies of Raymond were thrilled to get new and different styles of clothes for such a little amount of money, and it gave Gladys something to keep herself occupied.

CHAPTER 10

Gladys had just started her sewing business when, in April 1942, George was offered a full-time job at the lumber mill in Longview, Washington. He would be the head saw filer at the mill. His salary would be increased, and the mill supplied housing for the family.

With Trudy gone and Gladys still not warming up to Emma, and not having any close ties to anyone in Raymond now, they decided to take the job. Peter was not really happy about leaving his friends but knew that he would make new friends in Longview. Longview was situated on the Columbia River, a little west of Vancouver, Washington. The mill was much larger than the one in Raymond. A lot of the logs and milled lumber were sent by cargo ship down the west coast of the United States to ports along the California coast. Because of the fear of a Japanese attack along the West Coast, the cargo ships were heavily guarded and were escorted by the Navy and Coast Guard.

George, Gladys, and Peter moved the first week in May. George was sorry to leave his brother in Raymond but was moving closer to his brother in Portland. Charles Taylor, his wife Gwen, and their infant son lived in Portland. Charles worked in the shipyards on the Willamette River, doing the electrical work on newly built ships. His work was vital to the defense of the country, so he was exempt from the draft. George was looking forward to seeing his brother again. It had been over 10 years since he had seen him, and he had yet to meet Gwen.

The house that the Taylors were assigned was small but more than adequate for their needs. It had been closed up for several months, and when Gladys first went in, she opened all of the windows to air it out. The most horrible smell came into the house, and she immediately closed the windows and wondered what had happened.

The neighbor, Jane Longholt, came running over to the front porch just as Gladys was coming out the door.

"I was going to try and catch you before you went in and let you know that the paper mill in Camas is running today and the smell is terrible. When the wind blows to the west, the rotten egg smell of the mill blows into Longview. By the way, I am Jane Longholt. I live next door. I was hoping someone would move into this house soon. It gets lonesome with no other women around."

"I am Gladys Taylor. My husband is George, and my son is Peter. Thank you for warning me about the smell. It is really terrible," Gladys stated. "Is it that way all of the time?"

"No, only when the wind is blowing from the east. Camas is upriver from us, and when the wind blows downriver, it gets bad. Otherwise, this is a lovely town to live in. The people are friendly and very helpful. Of course, the security is super high everywhere we go because we are so close to the coast. The Coast Guard does patrol along the river all of the time, so it makes us feel a little safer," Jane explained. "I had best get home. Dinner needs to be started, and John will be home soon. Come over sometime if you get lonesome. I will introduce you to some of the other ladies in the neighborhood."

Gladys went inside to unpack some of her kitchen boxes. She was enjoying being able to put her own things away in the places she wanted them. She had never really been able to do that. On the farm, her mother had a place for everything, and Gladys kept things the same. As it was, most of the kitchen items that she had were originally her mother's. After she was finished with the kitchen, she made the beds and put Peter's clothes away in the closet and dresser.

"Mom," Peter hollered as he ran in the door. "Mom, where are you?"

"I am in the bedroom," Gladys answered back.

"Mom, I just met two guys who live down the street. They go to the same school I will go to. They like to play basketball the same as me. They invited me to go to the playfield at school and shoot some hoops with them. Can I go? Please!" Peter begged.

"Yes, you can go, but please be home by five o'clock. Your dad will be home by then, and we will have supper shortly thereafter. Tomorrow we will go to the school and register you for classes."

"Thanks, Mom," Peter said as he was running back to where the boys were waiting.

Gladys had a smile on her face as Peter was running off to be with his new friends. She was so glad that her son had made friends already.

Gladys had made some macaroni with a cheese sauce over it. Along with bread and butter and jelly that Gladys had made last summer, it was a good meal for their first night in their new home.

George walked into the house just as Peter was running out to meet his new friends. "I have our ration book for this month, so I can take you shopping tomorrow. I do not have to start work until Monday, so I have a couple of days to get us settled and to become familiar with the town," George explained when he came into the house. He had been out familiarizing himself with the housing area.

"We need to get Peter registered for school tomorrow so he can start on Monday. You heard how excited he was about meeting the boys today. I am glad he has made some friends. It will make it a lot easier for him to transfer schools," Gladys said.

After supper, Gladys cleaned up the kitchen, then joined George and Peter in the living room to listen to the news on the radio. It was not good news from Europe, but there had been some small victories in the Pacific, and it gave people a sense of hope.

George's work was much the same as in Raymond, except that the mill only worked two shifts, and he worked the swing shift and got home around 11:30 PM. Gladys didn't mind the hours because she was able to spend time with him in the mornings, but Peter didn't like his dad's hours at all. The only time he got to see him was on the weekends. George missed his basketball games and many of the school functions.

When school was out in June of 1942, the Taylor family made a trip to Portland to visit George's brother, Charlie, and his family. Gladys was again hesitant about meeting Gwen. She was afraid she would be like Emma and be cold and condescending to her.

Gladys was pleasantly surprised by Gwen's reaction. She was very open and affectionate and accepted Gladys as a member of the family immediately. They had a baby, Frederick, who was just 6 months old, and Gwen looked up to Gladys as an expert in child-rearing.

After a weekend in Portland, Gladys was very pleased to get back to her home in Longview. The summer promised to be a busy one.

Peter spent his time at the pool swimming or on the basketball court shooting hoops with his friends. George spent his weekends puttering around the house. He built several pieces of furniture for their use. He built both Peter's and Gladys's dressers for their clothes storage and built a nice table and four chairs for the kitchen eating area. George proved to be a very good craftsman. Gladys was happy with her little house and with having her own things around her. Even with the rationing, she enjoyed being creative in her kitchen.

Because of the rationing of gasoline for the car, they were not able to make another trip to Portland. George had to have the gasoline to get back and forth to work. They were able to make a short trip to the beach at Long Beach, Washington, and loved it there. Peter was able to fly a kite for the first time.

In the summer of 1943, the Allies were fighting in North Africa and making some headway. On September 3, 1943, the U.S. Army invaded Italy. That was good news for everyone at home because it meant some headway toward winning the war.

Peter started school again and enjoyed his 8th-grade year at Longview Elementary School. He was on the basketball team, and he liked to run on the track team.

In October of 1943, George was offered a job at the mill in Garibaldi, Oregon, on the coast. Gladys was not sure she wanted to live right on the beach, but George thought the opportunity would be a good one.

"Garibaldi is just north of Tillamook, Oregon, and south of a beach called Rockaway. I think we should check it out. It might be a great place for us to live. Also, they would guarantee that we would stay there for a few years and not have to move again soon. They are in the process of increasing the production of the mill. The lumber is being shipped out all along the West Coast of North America," George explained. Also, Peter would start high school there and most likely be able to finish there.

"Okay, we will move again. It would probably be best for Peter to be able to spend all four years of high school in one town and school," Gladys conceded.

So, when school was out in the middle of May 1944, the Taylor family moved again. This time to Garibaldi, Oregon. Garibaldi was a fishing town with a population of about 3,500 people. Along with being a fishing town, it was a mill town. Logging was a huge industry in Oregon, and the mill was very busy all of the time.

Peter rode his bike around town and easily met some boys his age, about ready to start high school in the fall. They were standing outside the local drugstore on June 6th when they heard the radio broadcast the news that the Allies had landed on the Normandy coast in Northern France. All of them got excited and rode home to let their families know what had happened. There was great excitement in the homes of their beach town that evening. This invasion was the beginning of the end of Nazi Germany.

CHAPTER 11

The Taylor family had rented a small house in Garibaldi, moved in, and found a church they wanted to attend. George was very satisfied with his job and enjoyed visiting with his fellow workers. He met one man who quickly became a good friend. He was married and had two older boys. He and his family lived in Rockaway Beach, about 10 miles up the coast highway from Garibaldi. The boys did not go to the same school as Peter, but they liked each other and were also basketball players. Ralph and Hazel Johnson went to the same church that George and Gladys attended, and they would spend Sunday afternoons together, often joining each other for the afternoon meal.

Gladys also became acquainted with the owners of the fish market in town. Garibaldi had a large fishing fleet, and the boats would come up to the dock behind the market and unload their catch right into the display cases in the store. Georgianna, or Georgie for short, was the wife of the owner of the market and worked behind the counter helping the customers. She had one son the same age as Peter who worked with his dad on the dock unloading the boats.

One day when Gladys and Peter went into the store to see what was available for purchase, Georgie called her son Greg in to meet Peter. Greg asked if Peter could go out onto the dock to watch the next boat come in.

"Is it safe for him?" Gladys asked.

"Oh yes, they are perfectly safe. My husband is very strict about the safety on the dock. Greg, take him out to the dock and show him how we get the fish into the market," Georgie said.

"Thank you. Peter is very curious about everything," Gladys commented.

"So is Greg," Georgie answered. "We didn't want Greg to have to go to work this young, but with so many of our boys overseas in the war, we desperately needed the help. You don't suppose Peter would like a job after school and on Saturdays, do you?"

"I don't know what my husband would say. I know Peter would love it, but we want him to get as good an education as possible, and that means doing homework and studying hard. I will ask my husband though," Gladys remarked. "By the way, I am Gladys Taylor, and my husband is George Taylor. He is the new saw filer at the mill. We moved here from Longview. I am hoping that we can stay in one place for a while."

"I am Georgie Green, and my husband is Bob Green. We have owned the Crab Shack for about six years now. With the war on, it has been a challenge to keep it going. Fortunately, fish is not being heavily rationed, so we are able to sell out the daily catch almost all of the time," Georgie explained.

"I am very happy to meet you, Georgie," Gladys said with feeling.

"Mom, that is so neat to see the boats come in loaded with fish. They also bring crab in. We have to be very careful of Dad and the crab, don't we, Mom?" Peter said.

"My husband is deathly allergic to crab," Gladys explained to Georgie. "All other fish is just fine for him, and he loves it, but when he eats crab, his throat closes up and he can't breathe."

"We will have to make sure he gets no crab then," Georgie said.

"Mom, Greg's dad asked me if I would like to have a job. Can I, Mom? I would love to work out there. It really beats mowing lawns," Peter begged.

Both Gladys and Georgie laughed at Peter's comment. "I will ask your father this evening," Gladys answered Peter. "It will depend on whether you keep up with your schoolwork," Gladys remarked. "That has to be your first priority."

"I know that, Mom, and I will get it all done. But I really want that job," Peter answered her.

"Like I said, I will talk to your father," Gladys finally said firmly. "We must go now and get the rest of our shopping done. Georgie, it was so good to meet you. We will see you again soon."

Peter was a good son. He was almost always cooperative and gave George and Gladys no problems. He was a good student and a very good athlete. He wasn't always the best on the team, but always gave a good showing and played with his whole heart. The coach and all of his teammates liked him.

Peter and Gladys walked back to their house to put the fish in the refrigerator. George was there waiting for them. The son of the owner of the mill was killed in Italy, and the owner closed the mill for the day, so George was able to be at home. He had an idea that he wanted to talk to Gladys about and was anxious for her to get home.

"Dad, Mr. Green is the owner of the Crab Shack on the waterfront. Mom and I were just there, and he asked if I would like to have a job after school and on the weekends. Can I, please? I would love to work there, and I promise I will get all of my homework done and keep my grades up," Peter pleaded.

"What kind of work would you be doing?" George asked.

"I would be helping unload the fish from the boats and taking it into the store, putting it in the display cases, and getting it ready to sell. Mr. Green said that because most of his former employees are away at war, he really needs the help. Can I work there, please, Dad?" Peter asked again.

"Let me think about it, Peter. I might be needing your help also in a few months," George said.

Gladys was immediately worried that something was wrong with George. "What is it, George?" she worriedly asked.

"Nothing serious, dear," George reassured her. "Just an idea that I have and want to talk to you about."

"Peter, you go on now and let your mother and I talk a bit. I will decide on the job as soon as I discuss something with your mother," George said.

"Thanks, Dad! I am going out to shoot some hoops," Peter said.

"Gladys, I have a chance to buy a piece of property in town for a very good price. I would like to buy it and build a house for us. Peter and I could do most of the work. I would have to hire an electrician and a plumber, but I know that I can do the rest," George explained to his wife.

"What about a mortgage, George? I don't want to get into the same situation that we did on the farm and lose a house again. The thought of not being able to pay our bills is very scary," Gladys bemoaned.

"I agree with you, but I just think now is the time for us to set down some roots. I can get almost all of the lumber at cost. Ralph will help with the construction. He is a master carpenter, has built several houses, and knows the area very well and where to get supplies at a reasonable cost. I am a good carpenter and am willing to learn what I don't know," George commented.

"Let's look at the land at least and see if it is a piece of property that we would want to live on. What about Peter and the job he has been offered with the Greens?" Gladys asked.

"It is okay with me as long as he keeps up with his schoolwork," George answered. "Do you want to tell him?"

"No, I think you should let him know of your decision. It will make him feel better that way," Gladys answered. "It will be good for him to have some money of his own. I think I will request that he buy some of his own school supplies, and if he has enough, maybe some of his school clothes. He is getting so big that nothing fits him anymore," Gladys observed.

"I am very proud of Peter and his accomplishments. He is a good student and makes friends easily. That has served him well for as much as we have had to move in the last few years. I really wasn't sure how he would do when we left the farm," George said.

"Unfortunately, I was so scared, I didn't think too much about how you or Peter would feel. I still miss Missouri, but I am content now. I know that we would have been in more trouble than we were if we had stayed. I did not like Raymond or Longview, but I do like it here. We are on the way to making some good friends, and that is very gratifying," Gladys commented. "Let's go ahead and investigate the possibility of building a house. It would really be something if we could own our own home."

George called Peter into the house and told him that he thought it would be good for him to have the job on the dock working for Bob Green.

"Thanks, Dad! I will go and tell him now," Peter said excitedly.

"Wait a minute, Peter. We have something else to discuss with you," George said. He proceeded to tell him about wanting to build a house of their own and how they would go about it. "We would also like you to help purchase some of your school clothes with the money you make at the Crab Shack. Money will be tight for a while because of the cost of supplies to build the house, but if you help out with some of your expenses, that will take a little of the pressure off."

"That sounds great, Dad. It would be neat to have a house of our own. And sure, I will help buy some of my clothes for school. I really don't need much. Shoes are the biggest thing. My feet don't want to stop growing," Peter added with a chuckle.

All three of the Taylors inspected the piece of property that was being offered for sale and thought it would be perfect for their needs. It was a corner lot three blocks from the main highway through town. It was only about a mile from the mill and close enough to the high school for Peter to ride his bike or walk in bad weather. It was also only four blocks away from Peter's new best friend, Greg Green, and that made Peter very happy.

George and Gladys went to the First National Bank branch in Garibaldi to talk about the possibility of getting a home loan. George was nervous about asking for a loan because he had lost the farm in Missouri.

Jeremy Blair was the loan officer at the bank and stood up when George and Gladys walked into his office.

"Hello, Mr. Blair. I am George Taylor, and this is my wife, Gladys. We are here to inquire about a home loan. We would like to build a house on a piece of property on the corner of 6th and Ivy Street," George explained to Mr. Blair.

"Do you have the necessary paperwork completed and signed?" asked Mr. Blair.

"Yes. These are all of the forms that I believe you will need," George said as he passed the file to Mr. Blair.

Jeremy Blair took the file from George and looked through the papers. "These all seem to be in order. You must have done this before, Mr. Taylor. You have all the forms that we need. Usually, the client has something missing."

"No, I have never applied for a home loan before. I did some research and talked to a couple of friends to see what papers would be necessary," George explained.

Mr. Blair asked George and Gladys several questions about their work history and their credit history. George explained that in 1940, they lost a farm in Missouri due to their inability to produce a paying crop.

"Mr. Taylor, that was the situation all over the country in the 1930s. Farmers in the Midwest were not able to grow a crop because of the weather. We do not take that fact into consideration when considering people for a home loan. Their past history is not always the deciding factor in approval or denial of a loan. I base a lot of my decisions on work history and if the applicant is reliable in their jobs and is currently paying their bills on time," Mr. Blair explained to George and Gladys. "We have a committee who will review your application and make a decision soon. The process only takes about two days. I will call you with our decision. I am very happy to meet both of you."

"Thank you, Mr. Blair. We look forward to hearing from you," George answered. After shaking hands, George and Gladys left the bank.

Jeremy Blair called George the next afternoon to let him know that the bank had approved their home loan and they could go into the bank anytime to sign the papers. George, Gladys, and Peter were very excited about being able to own their own home. They did know that they had a lot of work to do before they could actually move into their home.

CHAPTER 12

Very soon after hearing that their loan was approved and the purchase of the land was finalized, George rented a machine to grade the land and get it ready to pour the foundation. The whole neighborhood turned out to see what was going on and to watch the procedure.

Gladys spent the time poring over house plans and trying to decide which of five different plans she wanted. All three of them finally settled on a simple one-story, three-bedroom house with a living room, dining room, and a kitchen with a small eating area attached. George was planning on building some of the furniture out of scrap wood from the construction of the house and some pieces that he could get at the mill.

George's brother Charles had some extra tools that he did not use and was willing to use his gas ration to take them to Garibaldi. Charles was an accomplished carpenter, as was George, and he was excited about the fact that George and Gladys were building a home and would be staying in the area. He missed his brothers a lot. Like Gladys, Gwen did not get along well with Emma, so they didn't see them often, but Charles still missed Dan. They were a close family.

After the property was graded and the foundation was poured, it had to cure for about two weeks before construction could start. Peter thought it was a long two weeks. He wanted to get busy and build the house.

George would work at the mill until 5:00 PM, come home, have a quick dinner, and go to the site to work for about two hours every evening. Several of the men he worked with would show up to help, and a couple of Peter's friends would come over to see what was happening and help keep the site clean. They stacked the scrap lumber and picked up the debris that built up around a construction site. They were very concerned about someone getting hurt on the piles of lumber or on nails scattered on the ground. The Taylor house was the first construction in town since the war started, and everyone was excited to see the progress.

George was anxious to get the house framed and the roof on before the weather turned wet and cold. He thanked God every day that the summer had been a mild one and he could get a lot of work done.

George was eligible for a one-week vacation in August and used that time to concentrate on getting as much work done on the house as possible. He was able to get the rooms lathed and plastered and ready for wallpaper or paint. That was going to be Gladys's job.

In any spare time they had, they scoured the coastal towns for thrift stores and places where they could find used furniture to refinish and reupholster. They found some good pieces of furniture, and with the pieces that George would build, they felt they were well on their way to having a fine home.

On April 12, 1945, the beach town of Garibaldi received word that President Franklin D. Roosevelt had died. They knew that he was not well and was under an enormous amount of stress and strain, but they were shocked at the news of his death. Many of the people in town did not know any other president. He had seen them through the Depression and almost four years of the war. The whole town was in shock. The mayor and city council announced that the schools would be closed the next day.

Peter and Greg went to work at the docks unloading the daily catch, but their hearts were not in the work. The boats had gone out early in the morning before news of the president's death, and the fish still had to be unloaded and put on ice in the store.

Harry Truman was now the president of the United States, and he was an unknown. People were not sure in what direction he would lead the country now and if he had the knowledge and ability to end the war. The Allies in Europe were marching into Germany, and it looked like the fighting was winding down. The troops had found some of the camps that the Germans had established to confine the Jews and were horrified at the conditions of the survivors. News spread around the world about these camps, but people found it hard to believe the news stories.

The little beach town of Garibaldi was so far removed from the war in Europe that all of the news was like a myth to them. The fighting in the Pacific was a lot closer, and they were much more aware of the activities going on there.

On May 7th, Germany surrendered, and there was much joy all over the world, but the United States still had to fight the war in the Pacific, and they had some big battles ahead of them before victory was achieved.

Both Gladys and George were afraid the war would continue and Peter would be drafted. As long as he was still in school and had not turned 18 years old, he was safe. Hopefully, the war would be over before he had to register for the draft.

In August 1945, George and Gladys moved into their new home. There were a few small things that still had to be finished, but they were thrilled with the results of their labors. The house was a good, solid structure and was a great addition to the neighborhood. All of the neighbors came with food and gifts for their new neighbors, and Gladys was reveling in the attention she was receiving. The ladies were marveling at her decorating skills and the fact that a lot of her furniture was from thrift stores. And it was all done on a very small budget.

The news that the United States had dropped two atomic bombs on Japan and that the Emperor had finally surrendered was greeted with great joy all over the world. The country was done with war. The city of Garibaldi was no different from all other cities in the United States. A big celebration was planned, and George and Gladys were thanking God that the war ended before Peter was called up.

Both George and Gladys were enjoying the friends they were making in Garibaldi. They visited Ralph and Hazel Johnson in Rockaway often, sharing meals and holidays with them. They also became good friends with the Greens, the owners of the Crab Shack. Bob Green was impressed with George's carpentry skills and hired him to do some work for him at the Crab Shack and in their home. They also shared meals with them and always spent the 4th of July holiday together. Bob was in charge of the fireworks over the bay, and it was always a very impressive show.

Peter was doing well in school. He made top grades and worked after school, on weekends, and holidays. The extra money that he made helped with school clothes and supplies. He would occasionally take a girl to the movies or out for a soda but had no steady girlfriend, which made Gladys happy. It was still hard for her to give up control of his activities and let him make his own decisions.

In October 1945, George received word at work that his friend Ralph Johnson had been in a bad auto accident. Ralph was taken to the hospital in Tillamook and then transported to the trauma center at Emanuel Hospital in Portland. George was in shock. He had just seen Ralph the day before in the lunchroom at the mill, and he was fine. He took the time off work and drove Hazel to Portland while Gladys stayed home and took care of the Johnsons' children. The accident had severed Ralph's spine, and he was a paraplegic. He could move his upper body, but from the waist down, he could not move at all. From that point on, the Johnsons' lives changed, and they had to learn to adapt to a new situation and new surroundings. Ralph could no longer work in the mill. Hazel did not work outside of her home, so she had no working history to fall back on.

George and Gladys helped as much as they could. George made some modifications to their home, but it was not easy for Ralph to get around in a wheelchair. After a large settlement from the other driver's insurance company, Ralph and Hazel bought a grocery store in Rockaway Beach that was easily accessible for Ralph and had a home built that was completely wheelchair accessible. Hazel learned to do the books, work a cash register, and stock the shelves when necessary. Ralph could sit behind the register and did most of the ordering. The Johnson boys all worked at any job that was needed in the store.

The Taylors and the Johnsons remained friends, but their time together was limited now. The store took up all of the Johnsons' time, even the children's. Their lives evolved around school and the store.

In 1946, when Peter was 15 years old, George started teaching him to drive. Both he and Gladys knew that life would never be the same. Once Peter could drive and get himself around without their help, he wouldn't need them as much. It was a fairly sad and depressing time for Gladys. She doted on Peter and was very protective of him. She tried very hard to let go but was having a hard time of it. She wanted to know where he was all of the time and was deathly afraid that he would get hurt and she wouldn't know about it. Ralph Johnson's auto accident brought that to the forefront for her. She knew it was fruitless to worry the way she did and pretty much resigned herself to being worried all of the time and to hold him close as long as she could.

Peter graduated from Garibaldi High School in June of 1949. He fully intended to go to college but was not sure where or what he wanted to study, so he made the decision to join the Navy. He knew that his mom would not like it at all and joined without saying anything to either one of his parents. He was to leave for basic training the first of September, so he had the summer to be at home and have some time with his friends and family.

"Peter, why did you sign the papers without talking to your dad and me? This is a big mistake," Gladys cried.

"Mom, I will get some excellent training from the Navy and maybe some direction as to where and what I want to do with my life. I don't want to waste my time in school without knowing what I want to study. And I will have to serve in the military at some point anyway. I wanted to join and have the opportunity to choose what I want to do instead of being drafted into the Army and being a foot soldier someplace. Also, I know you and Dad cannot afford to send me to college. I know I have good enough grades to qualify for some scholarships, but they will not cover the entire four years. With my service in the Navy, I will be eligible for the GI Bill and save us all some money and a lot of debt. I can work during school also, but I don't want to be a slave to work and have my grades affected," Peter tried to explain to his crying mother.

"Son, it appears that you have thought this out completely and your ideas are sound. I hate to see you leave home so soon, but I do agree with you about wanting to get the experience of the military behind you before you go to school. I am proud of you, Peter," George told his son.

Peter left in August for basic training in San Diego, California. After six weeks of training, he had two weeks' leave at home and then was sent to Kodiak, Alaska. Gladys and George were very excited to have him home for the two weeks. George didn't realize how lonely it could be around the house without a bunch of teenage boys running in and out. Gladys seemed to be depressed all the time that he was gone. It was going to take some time for her to adjust now that he was gone. She no longer had any control over his activities, and she didn't like it. Peter would always be her little boy.

Peter had hoped to be stationed aboard a ship and travel around the world a bit, but he was assigned to the procurement office at the Naval Base in Kodiak for the next five years.

On June 25, 1950, the North Korean army invaded South Korea, and the United States, through the United Nations, was involved in another war. The Kodiak Naval Operating Base on the island was an integral part of the security of Alaska and of the United States. Alaska was a territory of the United States, and the responsibility of protecting it fell to the U.S. Navy.

Peter was concerned that he would be transferred to someplace closer. The Navy was going to play a crucial role in the conflict and would be vital to the UN forces in South Korea. Peter could have been assigned to a ship that would be off the coast of Korea, but he was assigned to the procurement office on Kodiak and stayed there the entire five years of his enlistment. He had a vital job in helping to supply the Navy with what they needed to fight the war in Korea.

Peter was able to call his parents once a month and tried to take a month's leave every year to go back to Garibaldi for a visit. Most of his friends were either in college or in the military, so his visits were not as exciting as they could have been, but he was glad to see his parents and spend quality time with them.

"Dad, it is beautiful country up there. I would love to go back with you sometime and do some hunting and fishing," Peter told his dad. "You would love it there."

"It would be great if there wasn't a war raging. Are you ever in danger, son?" George asked. "Your mother worries constantly."

"There are some reconnaissance planes that fly over, and we know they are Chinese planes, but they don't bother us. We shine the spotlights on them, and they fly away pretty fast. They don't want to start a naval air war. They don't have much of a navy right now and would lose very badly, especially that far away from their home base. Our ships that are off the South Korean coast are too menacing. The North Korean troops do not spend a lot of time along the coast. If the Russians got involved, we would be worried. They have a large naval presence in the North Sea, but right now we are okay," Peter explained to both his mom and dad.

They were relieved that he was relatively safe where he was but still wanted him home as soon as possible. At least if he was stationed in the United States somewhere, they would feel better.

In July 1953, North Korea, South Korea, China, Russia, Japan, and the United States signed an armistice, effectively ending the fighting in Korea. The naval base on Kodiak Island went wild. They would still have alerts, but the intensity of the alerts would not be as great, and the troops would feel less stress without the fear of a possible invasion from Russia or China.

George understood that the armistice was not a peace treaty, but just an agreement to cease the fighting. Technically, the North and South Koreans were still at war, and the country was divided at the 38th parallel, but the United Nations was out of it for now.

The lumber mill in Garibaldi increased production again as it did after World War II. The troops would be coming home and would need lumber for new housing. As the mill did in Longview, the trains would come into Garibaldi empty and leave full of cut and finished lumber.

Peter's enlistment would be up in October 1953. He had made the decision while he was in Alaska to go to Humboldt State College in Arcata, California. Arcata was on the coast of Northern California, just across the bay from Eureka, California. He wanted to stay along the coast, and Humboldt State would give him a variety of courses to take. He would also be able to attend school using the GI Bill. He had been able to save a good portion of his pay while he was in the Navy and had a good nest egg, so he would not have to depend on his parents.

George and Gladys were not excited about him being that far away, but the Oregon colleges were more expensive and did not offer him the same opportunities as Humboldt State did.

CHAPTER 13

There was joy and sorrow in Garibaldi when Peter came home from Kodiak. He flew to Honolulu, Hawaii, and then boarded a plane for Portland. Unfortunately, on board the plane from Hawaii were the bodies of two fallen soldiers from Garibaldi. They were both killed during the last days of fighting in Korea. Since Peter was from the same city as these two boys, he was asked to escort them all the way to Garibaldi and to attend to the needs of the families until funeral arrangements could be made.

George and Gladys drove to Portland to meet Peter's plane with the intention of driving him home. They were not aware that Peter had to stay with the bodies until they reached Garibaldi and were turned over to the families. They were only able to see Peter from a distance. He immediately went to the rear of the plane to be with the two caskets that were being unloaded.

Both George and Gladys were sorry that they did not get to take him home, but they were very proud of him for stepping up to the job of being an escort. Gladys thought he looked very handsome in his dress blues.

Peter was present for both of the funerals in Garibaldi. He had the honor of helping to fold the flag and present it to the families. He was not going to start school until January 1954, so he had a couple of months to rest and visit with friends. A lot of his high school buddies were either away at school or in the military. Greg Green had gone from high school right to the University of Oregon in Eugene. Georgie, his mother, said that he would not be home until Christmas but asked Peter if he would like to work during the time he was home. They always needed the extra help. Instead of sitting around all day doing nothing, he went to work on the docks unloading the fish again. Only now he was a lot stronger and was able to work much faster than he had when he was a teenager.

Christmas was a joyous time in the Taylor household. All of Peter's close friends were home from school or on leave from the military, and there seemed to be a party every night. It was a sad time for Gladys. She knew her boy was leaving again and this time would probably not ever live at home again. He would find a girl, get married, and make a home of his own. She didn't like the idea, but she knew it was inevitable.

In 1952, George had purchased a used 1951 Ford Custom 4-door sedan. He was so proud of the car and took extra special care of it. Peter thought it was one of the prettiest cars he had ever seen and was anxious to get behind the wheel. But George was hesitant about giving him the keys. Besides his house, it was the biggest purchase he had ever made, and he didn't want anything to happen to it, so it wasn't until the last week that Peter was home that George consented to let him drive, and then only when George was in the car with him.

"George, do you suppose you could take some time off and we could drive Peter to school?" Gladys asked. "I would at least like to see where he will be living and the town he is living in."

"I will check with the boss and see if that's possible. I would like to go down the coast highway. We could visit the Redwoods along the way," George answered.

Peter was glad to spend the extra time with his parents and to see the rest of the Oregon Coast. He had only been as far as Newport and was anxious to see the rest of the state's coastline.

He had to report for registration on the 5th of January, and classes were to start the next Monday, so they planned to leave on the 27th of December. That would give them plenty of time to do some sightseeing along the way. George had never taken a vacation from work, and his boss gave him two weeks over the holidays.

The weather was cold and rainy all the way down the coast, and at times, the wind blew pretty hard. But with both George and Peter driving, the trip was not a very hard one. They stopped at all of the sights along the way and thoroughly enjoyed their walk through the redwoods.

Arcata was a pretty town across the bay from the larger city of Eureka, California. Peter liked the proximity to the water and loved the school campus. It wasn't large like the University of Oregon in Eugene or Oregon State College in Corvallis. It was easy to find his classes, and his dormitory was close.

While Peter was settling into his dorm room and exploring the campus, George and Gladys were exploring the city of Arcata. George found out that there was a lumber mill in town, and Gladys toured the shopping areas of the city.

After settling Peter in and saying their goodbyes, George and Gladys headed north toward Oregon and home. It was a sad, somber drive home. They didn't talk much, saying very little about Peter and the probability of him never living at home again. Gladys had tears running down her face for most of the trip home.

The house in Garibaldi was so quiet when they got there. There were no young people running in and out all the time, and Gladys was not making sandwiches or cooking meals for anyone but herself and George, and they didn't feel like eating much of what she cooked anyway. Most of it went out for the gulls along the waterfront.

Unknown to Gladys, George had inquired about the availability of a job at the mill in Arcata while they were there. They were in need of another saw filer and suggested that George apply for the job. If he did apply and was offered the job, they would have to sell their house and move to California. He knew that Gladys was very lonesome for Peter, but he wasn't sure how she would feel about leaving her home and friends in Oregon.

One Sunday afternoon, while Gladys was busy with the women's group at church, George went to visit Bob Green to discuss the possibility of a move with him.

Bob was sure that George would have no problem selling his house. There was a shortage of houses to purchase in both Rockaway and Garibaldi, so it would probably sell quickly. Dwight Eisenhower was president, and the economy was on the upswing. Bob would be very sorry to see the Taylors leave the area, but he knew that both of them wanted to be closer to their son. He suggested that George use his phone to call Peter in Arcata and discuss the possibility of a move with him.

Peter was thrilled with the idea of his parents moving to Arcata. He was not happy living in the dorm. He had enough of dorm living in the Navy, and he missed his mom's cooking. He told his dad that if he lived at home and saved the money it cost to live on campus, he could afford to buy a used car to drive back and forth to school. The GI Bill did not cover the cost of housing; that was paid by Peter. George hadn't even considered that when he was thinking about moving.

"Peter, don't say anything to your mother yet. She knows nothing of this. I have not discussed it with her. I know that she wants to be closer to you, but I don't know how she is going to feel about moving again and leaving all of her friends. I intend to talk to her this evening. I will let you know what we decide," George explained to his son. "I love you, Peter!"

"I love you too, Dad. Thanks!" answered Peter.

George was home when Gladys got back from church. He was sitting in the living room reading the Sunday paper.

"Want to come in and sit with me for a few minutes? I have something I would like to talk to you about," George asked.

Gladys walked into the living room with a quizzical look on her face. "Yes? I do need to fix dinner," she said.

"Sit down for a few minutes," George said as he patted the sofa beside him.

"What's going on?" Gladys asked.

"When we took Peter to school, I looked at the mill in Arcata. They told me that they needed another saw filer. I was wondering if you would like to move to Arcata and be closer to Peter," George asked his wife.

"Sure, I would like to be closer to him. I don't like having him so far away, but what about the house?" she asked.

"We would have to sell it. Would you be okay with that?" George asked her. "Bob thinks it would sell very easily. There is a shortage of good housing in both Garibaldi and Rockaway."

"Sure. I love this house and the fact that you built it for us, but I love my son more. What would Peter think of this idea?" Gladys inquired.

"I have talked to him, and he is all in favor of it. He doesn't like dorm living. He says it is too much like the Navy. And he misses your home cooking. He told me that if he lived at home, the money he saved on the room and board charges would be enough for him to buy a used car to get back and forth to school. I agree with him on that point completely," George explained.

"Oh George, I love the idea," Gladys said as she threw her arms around her husband's neck. "Thank you!"

So, George called the mill in Arcata and applied for the saw filer job over the phone. After a discussion with the foreman of the Garibaldi mill, the owner of the Arcata mill called George back and offered him the job at more money than he was making in Oregon.

With a job secured, George called a realtor in Garibaldi and put the house up for sale. Gladys went through the entire house and cleaned it from top to bottom. It was spotless when the realtor showed it to a prospective buyer for the first time. After being on the market for two weeks, the Taylors had an offer of only $1,000 less than what they were asking. After paying off the mortgage, they thought they would have enough to move and still have enough to put a good down payment on a place in Arcata. Gladys insisted that they hire a moving company to get their belongings to California. She did not want to pack and move their things herself.

After several goodbye parties and lots of tears and promises of letters and phone calls, George and Gladys headed south to Tillamook and then over to Highway 99 to head south. They wanted to take a different route through Southern Oregon, but would head west to the coast at Medford and into California from there. This time the trip was a joyous one, and both George and Gladys were full of enthusiasm about their move.

They stopped for the final night in Eureka. It was just across the bay from Arcata, but they were tired and didn't want to see Peter when they were not really alert enough to talk to him. They did call him from the hotel where they were staying to make arrangements to meet for breakfast the next morning.

Peter's roommate had a car, and they had driven around looking at houses and neighborhoods that Peter thought his parents would like. He would stay in the dorm until the end of May when school was out. It was all paid for, and he could not get any sort of refund if he moved out early. Peter had a list of places he wanted his folks to look at the next day.

They met at a diner in Arcata the next morning for breakfast. Peter was there first, and when he saw his parents come in, he got up and picked his mother up and swung her around. She hissed at him to put her down, but he just laughed and spun her around again. She was secretly thrilled at the attention from her son. After putting her down, he gave his dad a big hug and then sat down to order breakfast.

"Boy, it is good to see you two!" Peter announced. "You have no idea how excited I am to have you here. Mom, I miss your good cooking. Dorm food is lousy! The Navy fare was much better than the dorm food. It will save me a lot of money living at home. I will, of course, help you with some of the expenses. I saved most of my Navy pay for room and board, but will be able to save it along with helping you two out a bit."

"We are happy to be here, son," George said. "Did you have a chance to search out some houses for us to look at?"

"Sure did! Virgil and I went out several times. I am anxious for you to meet Virgil. He is a really great guy and has been a perfect roommate. We found five houses that we thought might be good for you to look at," Peter explained. Virgil also started school in January after being in Korea for two years. His parents live in Chicago, but he wanted to stay on the West Coast. He loves the ocean, loves to go deep-sea fishing, and wants to learn how to hunt."

Gladys was not saying much, just soaking in the pleasure of being with her son again. His enthusiasm was infectious, and she was happy they had made the decision to move again.

"Should we go look at some of the houses now, or do you have studying to do?" George inquired.

"I am free for the day, so yes, we can go look now. I have the list of addresses with me. Dad, I tried to find places about halfway between the mill and the college so neither of us would have too far to drive," Peter explained.

After a full day of looking at houses, George and Gladys found one house that they both liked. It was a three-bedroom house on a good-sized lot with a garage attached to the house. It also had a utility room off of the kitchen and no stairs to climb up and down. There was room in the utility room for Gladys to set up her sewing machine and have enough space to work. The stove and refrigerator were in fairly good condition and came with the house. That was a good thing because they left their kitchen appliances with the house in Garibaldi.

"Shall we make an offer on it?" George asked after Peter had gone back to his dorm and they had settled into the hotel.

"I think it would be a good place for us. Like Peter said, it is not far from either the lumber mill or the college and is in a decent neighborhood. It is also within walking distance to a bus line if I need it and close to the grocery store. I like it, George. Yes, let's put an offer on it," Gladys said.

"What would you think of offering the spare bedroom to Virgil to rent? He is probably as tired of dorm food as Peter is, and it would give him the opportunity to have his own room," Gladys asked.

"Why don't we wait and meet him first? I think it would be a bit presumptuous of us to offer him a place to live without meeting him. And we should probably ask Peter what he thinks also," George said.

"You're right. I was getting a little ahead of myself. I am just so happy that Peter wants to live with us again. I want to make him as happy as possible," Gladys answered.

"My dear, you have got to remember that this will be just temporary. Peter will eventually want to move out on his own. He will find a girl, fall in love, and want to get married. You can't expect that he will be around all the time. He has lived an independent life from us for a few years now, and when he finishes school, he will want to again," George tried to explain to Gladys. He was afraid that she was not listening, though. She was so wrapped up in having Peter under her control again that she could not see into the future.

George called Peter and let him know that they were going to make an offer on one of the houses they looked at.

"That is the one I was hoping you would choose, Dad. It is a good size, and the fact that it has no stairs for Mom to climb up and down is a real plus," Peter said. "Are you going to see the realtor tomorrow?"

"Yes. Mom and I would like to know if you and Virgil would like to join us for dinner tomorrow evening. We would like to meet him. You would have to pick the restaurant. We don't know any good places here yet," George asked Peter.

"Sure, Dad. No problem. I will check with Virgil and call you back. Good luck on the house. I'm sure there will be no problems," Peter answered.

When George hung up, he explained to Gladys what was going on. They called the realtor who had listed the house they were interested in and made an appointment with him for the next morning. Both of them were anxious to get the process rolling. They did not want to stay in the hotel any longer than was necessary. They knew that there would be some time before the sale of the house closed, but they were going to inquire if they could pay rent until that time. It would be so much more convenient than having to find a short-term apartment to live in.

All went well with the realtor. He was very excited to have the offer on the house. It had been sitting vacant for almost a year with no offers. He called the owners, and they were very agreeable to the idea of the Taylors paying rent while they were waiting for the sale to close. That meant that they could move in right away.

George called Peter to let him know about the sale and the fact that they would be moving in right away. He was very excited about the idea. "Dad, Virgil and I will meet you at the Harvest House Restaurant on 16th Street this evening for supper. It is a really good place to eat and fairly reasonably priced. And Dad, you can count on both of us to help with the moving in. See you later at the restaurant," Peter said as he hung up the phone.

CHAPTER 14

I am very glad to meet you, Mr. and Mrs. Taylor. Peter has told me so much about you that I feel I know you already, Virgil said as he shook hands with both George and Gladys.

"And we are very glad to meet you, Virgil. Please, let's sit down and order. I am starved. Peter says they have good food here," George responded.

"They certainly do. It is a treat for us to get away from dorm food. It really isn't the best, although it is 100% better than some of the stuff I got in Korea," Virgil added.

They all ordered and chatted for a while before their food was served. All four of them dug into their meals with gusto and finished with pie and coffee.

"Since today is Thursday, I will call the moving company and see if arrangements can be made for the truck with our belongings to be at the new house on Saturday morning. Hopefully, we can move in then. I am anxious to get out of the hotel," George mentioned.

"We will be more than happy to help with the move, Dad. It shouldn't take long to get everything into the house, and then we can start unpacking and putting stuff away," Peter added. "I know that Mom will want to change things around a hundred times before she is satisfied with the way it looks," Peter said as he grinned at his mother.

Gladys slapped her son on the shoulder playfully and said, "Don't tease me, Peter. I just want my home to look perfect."

Peter put his arms around his mother's shoulders and gave her a kiss on the cheek. "I know, Mom. Anywhere you make a home for us always looks perfect."

When George and Gladys returned to their room at the hotel, Gladys said, "George, I like that young man. Why don't you call Peter and ask him about Virgil renting the third bedroom from us? It would help us out financially and help him out by getting him out of the dorm. They are both paid up until school is out at the end of May. This is the first part of April. It would give us time to get everything in place in the house and used to living there."

Peter thought that it was a terrific idea, and when he talked to Virgil, he thought so also. The idea of trying to get a new roommate in the fall was not very exciting for him.

"I would not move in until September when school starts, though," Virgil said. "I am going to go home for the summer months. My dad is not well and needs some help around the house. I will be able to do some of the chores for him."

"That would work out fine. The only thing I think you would need to supply would be bedroom furniture. My folks have my bedroom furniture, but they don't have any extra," Peter explained.

"No problem. I can get that before I leave for Chicago," Virgil answered.

The only difficulty that any of them could see would be that there was only one bathroom in the house and they would all have to use it, but they would be able to adapt.

George started his new job at the mill the Monday after moving into their new home. It was somewhat chaotic for a few days, but Gladys dug in and got a lot of the boxes unpacked and things put away where she wanted them. Peter helped her for a little while in the evenings, but he didn't have a lot of time between classes and the studying he had to do.

George was adapting to his new job. He was the head saw-filer and was able to set the schedule as needed, but he did not change anything. He was very pleased with the way things were running now. The crew he was working with seemed to be very efficient and capable of doing an excellent job at sharpening the saw blades. He also noticed that their incident reports were very low, which was a plus in the crew's favor as far as he was concerned.

Once Gladys had the kitchen up and running, Peter and Virgil were over for supper as often as their schedules would allow. They both had a couple of night classes, so were not able to come for supper on those days. Gladys was thrilled to be cooking for Peter again.

School was out at the end of May. Virgil went home to Chicago to be with his parents, and Peter got a job at the mill stacking lumber. He found time to go fishing with some of his other friends, and occasionally, George went along.

The summer went by quickly. Virgil returned from Chicago at the end of August and moved into the spare room in the Taylor house. He had purchased a car, as had Peter, so there were three cars in the driveway. Virgil agreed to park his on the street so that there was not a hassle about moving cars in the early mornings when all three of the men had to be out of the house at different times.

Peter still hadn't declared a major and had taken mandatory courses his first year in order to graduate. He would have to declare a major in his sophomore year if he wanted to graduate in four years. He was taking some basic accounting courses the first semester of his sophomore year. He thought he might like to be an accountant. He had always been good with numbers and got top grades in all of his math classes.

As he was walking along the business street in downtown Arcata one day, he noticed a CPA's office. The 'Open' sign was showing, and he decided to go in and see if he could talk to the owner. He might get some information about the business to help him make a decision about a career.

As he walked into the office, he noticed that the receptionist was a very pretty girl. She was on the phone but indicated to him to have a seat and that she would be with him shortly. Peter sat in the chair in front of her desk and just looked at her. He was very impressed.

"Hi! I am sorry. I have been trying to get that lady off the phone for quite a while. She insists that I have to help her with her financial problems, but doesn't want to pay the fee. What can I do for you? Do you have an appointment that I don't know about?" she said as she looked at the appointment book on her desk.

"No, I don't. This might sound a little strange, but I am a student at the college and am taking some accounting classes. I have not declared a major yet and was thinking about becoming a CPA. I thought that if I could talk to someone in the business, it might help me make up my mind. Oh, by the way, my name is Peter Taylor."

"My name is Carrie Hunter. I will see if Mr. Bjorn has time to see you now."

After about fifteen minutes of talking to Mr. Bjorn, Peter decided that accounting would not be for him. The thought of sitting behind a desk all day working with numbers and never getting out to see people was not something he wanted to do with the rest of his life.

He thanked Mr. Bjorn with a handshake and left his office. Just because he didn't want to pursue a career in accounting didn't mean he didn't want to pursue a relationship with Carrie Hunter. He was quite taken with her.

"Would you consider having lunch with me someday?" Peter asked Carrie when he was ready to leave the office.

"Sure, I would like that. I have a 45-minute lunch, usually at 1:00 PM if you would like to come by. There is a good café just around the corner that I go to a lot," Carrie said.

"How about tomorrow?" Peter asked. "Okay,

see you at 1:00 o'clock," Carrie stated.

Peter didn't say anything to his parents or to Virgil about his lunch date with Carrie. He wanted to keep it under wraps for a while. He knew his mother would be upset if he had a girlfriend. His dad would ask him if he had a girlfriend yet, and his mother would pipe in with, "Oh George, he has a lot of time for that yet. He doesn't need to complicate his life with a girl now. Anyway, he is too young to become serious about anyone."

Peter would look at his dad with a sad look on his face. He wanted to share with his family that he had met a girl that he liked a lot.

Carrie was 22 years old and from Nebraska. She lived with her sister and her family here in Arcata. She had gone to school at Humboldt State for two years but had to drop out to work. She couldn't afford to go any longer. She was working at the accounting firm to save money to continue with school.

He had had several dates with Carrie by now and really liked her, and it seemed the feeling was mutual. She was fun to be with and liked a lot of the same things he did. She loved to fish, although the limit of her experience was fishing in the stream that ran through her parents' property.

Carrie's parents had managed to hang onto their farm during the Depression, but just barely. Her two brothers were running it now and doing fairly well. They raised wheat and corn and had been able to pull in decent crops for the last few years. They raised a few beef cattle, mostly for local use.

Carrie didn't like the farm life. She was a city girl. She loved going to San Francisco but couldn't afford to very often. It was a real treat when she and her sister would go. Her sister's husband was an attorney, and they had a pretty nice house in the hills above Arcata.

George had a feeling that Peter had a girlfriend. He was out late on Friday and Saturday evenings and had a special look about him most of the time. George was sure it was the look of a man falling in love.

Gladys was sure that Peter did not have a girlfriend. She thought he was out with Virgil and some of their other friends.

On a Thursday evening at dinner, Peter asked his mother if it would be okay to invite one of his friends over for dinner on Saturday evening.

"Of course, dear. You are always welcome to invite some of your friends over. I would appreciate meeting some of the other fellows you run around with. Virgil is the only friend that I have met," Gladys answered.

On Saturday evening, Peter walked into the house with Carrie Hunter, and Gladys about fell over. She had no idea that the friend Peter wanted to invite over was a girl. She was polite but noticeably cold when she greeted Carrie. George was impressed with Carrie and liked her immediately.

The meal was a little tense, but Carrie handled herself extremely well. She complimented Gladys on a very delicious meal and tried to engage her in conversation several times, but Gladys only gave one or two word answers to Carrie's questions or comments.

After dessert, Peter, who was very disappointed with his mother's actions, took Carrie home. When he arrived back at his parents' home, he was visibly upset with his mother.

"Mom, you were very rude to Carrie. I have never seen you rude to a guest in our home before. What in the world was wrong?" Peter asked his mother.

"Why didn't you tell me that it was a girl that you were bringing home? You are not ready for a steady girlfriend yet. You know how I feel about that," Gladys answered back.

"Mom, I like her. She is fun to be with. We like a lot of the same things. She was raised on a farm in Nebraska and comes from basically the same background as I do. What in the world is wrong with that? I am 24 years old for heaven's sake. I certainly am old enough to have a girlfriend. I am not going to marry her this weekend, for God's sake," Peter said in a heated voice as he walked down the hall to his bedroom.

About that time, Virgil came in from his date, noticed the tension in the room, and headed straight for his room.

"George, I do not like her, and I do not approve. Please see what you can do about stopping this relationship now," Gladys begged her husband.

"No, I will not interfere, Gladys. I think Carrie is a lovely girl. She is the first real girlfriend that Peter has had. You have chased all the others away. Let him make his own decisions. He is old enough to date whomever he wants to without his parents interfering. I think you need to loosen up and get to know the girl. You might surprise yourself and like her."

CHAPTER 15

Gladys was crushed. Logically, she knew that Peter would find someone to spend the rest of his life with, but she wasn't ready for that yet. He had not said that he was going to marry this girl, but from the looks he gave her, he was getting serious about her.

"Mama, she is from the Midwest, like we are, and she grew up on a farm. Her parents were able to hold onto their farm during the Depression, but it was not easy for them. Her dad had some friends and family who helped them out. Carrie has two sisters and two brothers. Both of her brothers live and work on the farm. One sister lives in Lincoln, Nebraska, and her younger sister lives here in Arcata. She is just a good down-to-earth Midwest girl," Peter tried to explain to his mother.

Gladys knew that it would take some time to get used to not being the only woman in her son's life. She was going to try hard not to alienate Peter completely, but she didn't like it.

George was happy for Peter. He wanted him to find someone that he could love and be loved in return. He had hoped that he would finish school first, but maybe he would wait to get married. Maybe Carrie was not the one for him, but at least he had some female companionship.

Carrie came for dinner again the next weekend. When dinner was over, she offered to help clean the table off. Gladys immediately said no, that she would do it herself. Carrie recoiled a bit, as did Peter and George. They retired to the living room to listen to the radio news while Gladys cleaned up the kitchen. Carrie stepped back into the kitchen for a moment to say goodbye and thank Gladys for the meal, then Peter took her home.

George walked into the kitchen after they left and looked at Gladys with an odd look on his face. "Gladys, listen to me!" he stated. "You know you sounded just like Emma when you spoke to Carrie right after dinner. She was gracious enough to offer to help you, and you turned her down just like Emma did to you. That was totally unfair and not like you at all. You might not like the girl, but that is no excuse for being rude to her or to Peter."

George turned around and left the kitchen. Gladys was stunned. He had never talked to her like that before. George never really got angry, but he was angry with her now. She sat at the kitchen table for a while, drinking a cup of tea and remembering back to how she felt when they first came to the West Coast in 1940 and how scared she was to meet Emma, and how upset she was at the rebuff Emma gave her when she offered to help clear the table after supper that first evening.

She concluded that George was right. She was very rude to Carrie. She loved her son so much and wanted to keep him with her as long as possible, but she knew that she would have to let go sometime. She just didn't want him to get hurt, and she was afraid that Carrie Hunter would hurt him.

When Peter got home from Carrie's, he went directly to his room to study. He had a huge test coming up on Monday and had to be ready for it. He had spoken briefly to his dad but had not seen his mother. She was still sitting in the kitchen, not ready to approach George yet.

"Did I hear Peter come in?" Gladys asked George as she walked through the living room, headed for the hallway.

"Yes. He is studying for a test he has on Monday," George answered without looking up at her.

"Thanks," Gladys said as she proceeded to knock on Peter's door.

"Come in, Mother," Peter said as Gladys opened the door. "I have a big test on Monday and need to get this studying done. I will probably be at the books all day tomorrow also, so don't expect me to be of much help around here."

"I just wanted to apologize for my behavior tonight. It was unkind to both you and Carrie. I am very sorry," Gladys pronounced.

"It is not me you need to apologize to; it is Carrie. She was hurt, and frankly, I wouldn't be surprised if she didn't want to see me anymore. I am very disappointed, Mom. That was not like you and reminded me of all those years ago when we first arrived in Raymond and Aunt Emma treated you that same way," Peter stated.

"Your dad said the same thing, and I agree with you. I am terribly sorry for what I said. If you will give me her address, I will write her a note of apology," Gladys added.

"Thank you, Mom. I love you and don't want to be angry or upset with you, but you really surprised me this evening," Peter said as he smiled at his mother.

After Gladys left Peter's room, she went to talk to George.

"I want to explain to you how I feel, George. I am terribly afraid that I will lose Peter completely if he finds a girl to marry and love. He is my only child, and I do not want to lose him or his love. I don't think I could bear not having him in my life anymore," Gladys said.

"What makes you think that Peter would love you any less if he were married?" George asked. "You will always be his mother, and he will always love you. You cannot hide him away from life all the time, my dear. He needs to have both male and female friends. It is a part of life. I did not love my mother any less when I married you," George explained.

"Yes, but your mother had other children. I don't! Peter is the only one," Gladys cried.

"I know that, Gladys. And I am sorry that we didn't have a houseful of kids, but it just didn't happen. We were blessed with only Peter. But we could have a houseful of grandkids if you let go a little and give him some space. Just think, Dan and Emma have no children and no one to carry on the name," George explained.

"I have told Peter that I would write Carrie a note of apology. I think I will get to that right now," Gladys stated.

Carrie received the note of apology from Gladys on Wednesday. She had not spoken with Peter since then. She knew he had a lot of studying to do that week with several exams coming up.

Peter called her briefly on Wednesday evening, asking for a date on Friday evening. She let him know that she had received a note from his mother and yes, she would like to see him Friday evening, but she was scheduled to work on Saturday, so had to make it an early evening.

Occasionally, Mr. Bjorn would schedule clients to come in on Saturdays when they couldn't make weekday appointments, and he liked to have Carrie in the office in case he needed additional information. She never minded working on Saturday. Mr. Bjorn paid her time and a half when she did, and the extra money always came in handy.

Gladys had asked Peter to bring Carrie by the house on Friday evening. Peter was a little reluctant to do that but finally agreed because of the pressure of one of his mom's chocolate cakes.

Gladys was very contrite when Peter and Carrie showed up on Friday evening. She apologized to Carrie again for her actions the last weekend, and all seemed to be well between them.

Gladys was surprised that Carrie had to work on a Saturday. "Once in a while, Mr. Bjorn has a client who cannot make an appointment during the week, and he schedules a Saturday appointment. He likes to have me on hand unless the phone rings or he needs additional information. And I get paid time and a half for working on the weekend, so that doesn't hurt either," Carrie explained.

As Peter and Carrie were getting ready to leave, Gladys gave Peter a brief hug and shook Carrie's hand, saying, "Again, please excuse my horrible behavior of last weekend. I hope that you will come back again soon."

When Peter came home from Carrie's, he realized that his parents had gone to bed, so he turned off the lights and headed toward his room. As he passed his parents' room, he heard them arguing. It was very rare that they ever argued. His dad was a pretty mild-mannered person and usually let his mom rant and rave until she had played out her anger, then talked to her calmly. This time was different. He was actually arguing with her.

"I just don't like her, George. She is much too sophisticated for Peter. She is going to want expensive things, and he won't be able to provide them for her; then she will find someone else who will," Gladys said. "She is going to hurt him, George. I can feel it in my bones."

"I will be very sorry if she does, Gladys, but that is Peter's business, and he is the one who will have to decide what to do about it. It is not up to you or me," George tried to explain.

"I have always taken care of him. He is my son!" Gladys announced firmly.

"Gladys, he is a grown man now. He can take care of himself and make his own decisions. He does not need his mama's help. And for your information, I like her a lot, and I think she would be very good for him!" George declared.

Peter sighed and walked down the hall to his room. George and Gladys were not aware that he had heard part of their conversation.

Peter tried to study for his exams coming up, but his mind was on Carrie and his parents. He was very sad that his mother didn't like Carrie. He knew that she was very possessive of him and wanted to protect him, but he didn't realize that it would be to the exclusion of other females in his life. He had never really had a steady girlfriend before. He dated a lot in high school but never one girl on a regular basis.

Peter loved his mother dearly and wanted to please her, but he also wanted a life of his own. He liked the fact that he was living with his parents because he was saving a lot of money, but he didn't like the restrictions of living under the same roof as his mom. It was like having a monitor on him all the time. He was falling in love with Carrie and wanted to explore a future with her, but how could he be comfortable with her and have his mother feel the way she did?

At breakfast on Saturday morning, Peter asked his dad to help him pick out a new pair of boots at the sporting goods store in Eureka.

"Your dad has a lot of things to do today, Peter, and doesn't have the time to go shopping. I will be happy to help you pick out a pair of boots," Gladys announced.

"I kind of wanted Dad's opinion, Mom. It can wait until you have more time," Peter said as he looked at his dad.

"It's okay, Peter. I have the time to go with you this morning. The chores I have to do aren't so urgent that I can't spend some time with my son," George said.

"George, you have to clean and rehang the screens on the north side of the house. I would really like them done today," Gladys said firmly.

"I will get them done in my own good time, Gladys. I am going to the sporting goods store with Peter," George reiterated.

"But, George. You know that shopping is not your thing," Gladys started to say.

"Gladys, no further discussion is necessary. I am going shopping with Peter, and that is final. I will get the screens washed and rehung; if not today, then tomorrow."

"Peter, I'll meet you at the car in a half hour," George said firmly, all the while giving Gladys a look of defiance.

"Thanks, Dad. I'll be ready," Peter said as he headed down the hallway to his room.

After making the arrangements with Peter, George followed Gladys back into the kitchen. "Why is it that you don't want me to go shopping with Peter? You know nothing about men's boots. What makes you think that you can be more help to him than I can?" asked George.

"I wanted to talk to him about Carrie. I don't think that she is good for him, George. I am sorry, but she is a social climber and will want more from him than he is able to give," Gladys said.

"You sure don't have much faith in Peter, do you? Just drop it, Gladys. Let Peter make up his own mind. If he gets hurt, so be it. I will not like it any better than you will if that happens, but he has to make his own choices. Just leave him alone," George demanded.

"You just don't understand!" Gladys cried at him and left to head to their bedroom.

All the while the conversations were going on about Peter and Carrie, Virgil was in and out of the house. He was embarrassed to be a witness to the arguments between George and Gladys and felt sorry for Peter having to go through all of this. He appreciated not having to live in the dorm, especially since he was older than most of the students there, but he wasn't sure he wanted to live amid all of the tension in the Taylor household either. Life could sure get complicated sometimes.

Peter and George went on their boot-buying trip to the sporting goods store in Eureka, then went for a cup of coffee.

"Peter, I want you to know that I like Carrie a lot. She is a lovely girl. Are you serious about her?" George asked.

"I am, Dad," Peter answered. "I am falling in love with her, and she says she feels the same about me. We are going to take it slow, though. I need to get farther along in school and closer to a career before we make any kind of commitment to marriage. She wants to work a bit longer, save some more money, and go back to finish her degree. She is a good accountant but needs that degree to get a good job."

"Please try and be patient with your mom. She has always been so protective of you and will most likely find fault with anyone you choose as a partner. No one is going to be good enough for you. You will always be her little boy, no matter how old you are," George tried to explain.

"I know, Dad, but I don't feel comfortable bringing someone home when she is rude to them. I know she wrote Carrie a note of apology, but I also know that the note was only for her actions, not what she thought about her. She acted just like Aunt Emma did when we first arrived in Raymond. I was young, but I remember how uncomfortable Mom was being there," Peter explained.

When they got home from their shopping trip, Peter bypassed the living room and went right to his room to put his boots away and get busy with the studying he still had to do.

George walked into the living room and found Gladys lying down on the sofa with her eyes closed, listening to the Boston Pops Orchestra on the radio. She wasn't aware that George had come into the room. He went over to her and put his hand on her shoulder. She was startled by his touch. "I didn't hear you come in the room," Gladys mumbled, closing her eyes again. "I was just lying here enjoying the music and guess I fell asleep. I will get up and fix you supper."

"It isn't suppertime yet, dear. Are you not feeling well?" George inquired with concern.

"I have a slight headache. I took some aspirin, but it hasn't worked yet," Gladys responded.

"You rest, and I will get busy on the screens," George said. He walked into the kitchen and noticed that the breakfast dishes were still on the table and nothing had been put away. He was surprised because Gladys was usually religious about cleaning up the kitchen after a meal.

CHAPTER 16

Peter had taken one summer school class in psychology and enjoyed it very much. He thought he might talk to the psych department counselor and see what it took to become a school counselor. He found he liked working with young people at the high school level. He had been a tutor on Kodiak Island while he was stationed there in the Navy. Some of the civilian personnel had their families with them, and the children needed tutors to keep up with their studies.

A school counselor was a career that he felt he would enjoy. This summer school course that he was taking was an introduction to that major. Peter found it very interesting and challenging.

He would have to declare a major course of study during the fall semester. He talked to Carrie about it, and she thought that he would be good at advising the kids both about school and personal issues. Peter valued her opinion but decided to talk to some of the high school counselors in the Arcada and Eureka school districts. He called the offices of both districts, explained why he wanted to talk to the counselors, and was given the contact numbers for each high school in both districts.

"Carrie, I was able to get appointments with five counselors. When I called, one of the longtime counselors at Arcada High School said that it was the first time he had ever been approached by a prospective student who wanted to major in school counseling," Peter explained. "I sat and talked to him for two hours."

Peter proceeded to explain to Carrie that the man said he needed to have good listening, observational, and communication skills; that he had to be compassionate and kind and be able to share and laugh at the stories the students would tell.

"I would have to have a bachelor's degree in either school counseling, psychology, social work, or education. Then I would have to go on and get a master's degree in school counseling and serve an internship. It would be a long haul, but I think it will be well worth the time and money. What do you think?" Peter asked Carrie. "Would you be willing to put up with me going to school for that long?"

"Sure, but are we going to be together for that long?" Carrie asked.

"I sure hope so. I love you, Carrie, and want nothing more than to marry you and build a life together," Peter said. "Will you marry me, Carrie?" he asked as he put his hands on her shoulders and pulled her close. "I don't have a ring for you, but maybe we can pick one out together if you say yes," Peter said with a hopeful tone to his question.

"Yes, Peter, I will marry you. I love you and want nothing more than to share your life with you and have your babies," she answered. "The only problem would be your mother's reaction. She does not like me, and that is very evident every time I am around her. What will you do if she objects, which she will?"

"I love my mother, and I know she feels that only she knows what is best for me, but I don't want to marry my mother. I want to marry you. Mother has no say in who I do or don't marry. That decision is mine and yours to make on our own," Peter stated very firmly.

Carrie had to get back to work after a longer-than-usual lunch break. She was sure her boss would understand after she told him why she had been gone so long.

Peter wasn't so sure about his mother. He was thinking he wouldn't say anything until his dad got home and they sat down to dinner. He wanted his dad there when he told his mother that he was marrying Carrie Hunter. Peter knew that he would get a negative reaction to the news and needed his dad there for moral support.

Virgil was due back in town in another week. Peter would be glad to have him back. Virgil was a good buffer between his mother and himself. He was able to calm Gladys down in a way even her husband could not.

Dinner that evening started out very quietly. Gladys had baked some fish and had a salad to go with it. She had made some banana pudding for dessert, and it was over dessert that he announced to his parents his impending marriage to Carrie Hunter.

His dad sat eating his pudding with a big smile on his face and said, "Congratulations, son. I am very happy for you. Carrie is a fine woman and will make a good wife for you."

As George was speaking, he turned to Gladys and was shocked at the look on her face. It was a look of horror.

"Peter, I will not let you do this," Gladys announced with force. "You would be making the biggest mistake of your life if you marry that girl. She is not worthy of you. She is the type of girl who will bleed you dry. She will take and take from you and give you nothing back. I just forbid you to do this foolish thing!"

Both George and Peter looked at Gladys with shocked expressions on their faces.

"Mother, you cannot forbid me to do anything. I am 24 years old and am able to make my own decisions. I love Carrie Hunter and I will marry her. I'm sorry you do not like her because she is an outstanding person.

Now, I am going to lay down some rules, and if these rules are not followed, I will find other living arrangements," Peter explained. "First, if I bring Carrie here to this house, you will be polite. You will say nothing negative to her or about her to anyone."

"If I hear anything negative about her coming from your mouth, I will move. I promise you that. I do not like talking to you this way, Mom, because I love you, but I will stick to my guns on this matter. I love Carrie Hunter and will marry her."

George commented to Peter, "I am very happy for you, Peter. I think you have made a great choice of a life partner. I know you will be very happy."

Gladys said nothing. She got up from the table and left the room, heading for the living room and the radio to listen to the Boston Pops Orchestra. That seemed to be her escape. Peter went into his room to figure out the classes he would take this fall. After talking to the counselors and to Carrie, he was sure that being a school counselor was what he wanted for his career. He was sure that his dad would agree, but he was not sure about his mom.

George thought that Gladys was acting especially strange lately. She had been very possessive about Peter from the time he was first born, never wanting him very far from her sight and always directing and dictating his activities. But as he got older and more independent, she was getting worse. It seemed she was having a hard time realizing that he was a grown man with his own life to live and his own decisions to make. If they turned out to be the wrong decisions, that was his problem.

George was also concerned about his wife because it seemed she was having more headaches lately. He needed to get her to a doctor for a checkup, but she was reluctant to go, always finding an excuse for not going. Her actions were strange, too. She was not cleaning up the kitchen, and she had forgotten several times that she had things on the stove cooking. She had almost burned several of their meals lately.

"Gladys, I need to talk to you. Gladys!" George called to her, but she did not pay any attention to him. She only listened to the music on the radio. George went over to the radio and turned it way down.

"I was listening to that. Turn it back up, please," Gladys demanded.

"I want to talk to you, Gladys, and I can't talk over the noise of the Boston Pops," George explained.

"Not now, George. I have a headache and want to listen to the music."

George turned the radio off. "Now, Gladys. I am sorry you have a headache, but we need to talk about Peter and about your health," George said sternly. "First of all, you are going to push Peter completely away with your attitude about Carrie. He loves her and is going to marry her whether you like it or not. If you want continued contact with your son, you are going to have to change your attitude."

"I will not change my opinion of that girl. She is not good for him. She will hurt him and bring him nothing but trouble," Gladys emphasized.

"You do not know that, Gladys. She is a very nice girl and loves your son, and he loves her. She is smart, has a good job, and will support Peter's ambitions in any career he chooses to go into. Be grateful, Gladys, please!" begged George. "Tomorrow, I am going to make an appointment with Doctor Powers for you, and I will take you in to see him."

"No! I do not need to see a doctor. You cannot make me see him," Gladys cried.

"Why are you so afraid to see Doctor Powers, or any doctor?" asked George.

"I told you, I don't need a doctor. I absolutely refuse to go. I don't want to discuss it any further. Please turn the radio back on. I want to listen to the rest of the program," Gladys demanded.

When her program was over, Gladys got up and went into the bedroom to get ready for bed. She lay down and was asleep in minutes.

George went into the kitchen to put the leftover food away and wash the dishes. This made the fourth night in a row that Gladys had not cleaned up the kitchen, and she was usually so religious about doing it right after dinner. Something other than Peter's situation was going on with her, but if she wouldn't go to a doctor to find out, he was at a loss as to what to do for her.

Gladys had not made any good friends since they had moved to Arcada. They had joined the Baptist Church, but she had not participated in any of the activities yet. She had been invited to the women's Bible study group and to the social time after service on Sunday, but had opted not to go. George would have liked to have a cup of coffee with the members after church, but went ahead and left with Gladys. Her only comment was that none of the ladies interested her. Maybe someday!

CHAPTER 17

George made an appointment with the doctor and went to see him to talk about Gladys and what was going on with her. The doctor could not talk specifically about Gladys but did say it sounded like she might be depressed and maybe needed a general checkup and to be put on some antidepressants. But there was nothing he could do if she was not willing to come in to see him.

George left feeling as helpless as he did before he saw the doctor. If she wouldn't go see him, there was nothing he could do.

Most of the time, Gladys just sat and listened to the radio. She took no interest in doing any housework or cooking. More often than not, George came home to find supper had not been started and Gladys taking a nap. She constantly complained of a headache but would not take an aspirin for it. She said it would go away if she could sleep it off. If she wasn't sleeping, she was listening to the radio.

Peter tried to talk to her, but she just said that he had betrayed her and didn't want to listen to him. She had effectively cut her family out of her life.

Virgil returned to Arcada from his summer with his family. He was shocked when he saw Gladys. She had lost weight and took no care in her personal appearance.

"What has happened?" Virgil asked Peter.

"It started the first time Mom met Carrie. She detests her and thinks I have betrayed her by wanting to marry Carrie. I know she has always thought that she knew what was best for me, but this time she is wrong. I am going to marry Carrie Hunter no matter what my mother says," Peter explained.

"That doesn't sound like the Gladys I know," Virgil exclaimed.

Virgil soon realized that a hot supper was not something he was going to get at the Taylor house. He told Peter that he was thinking of getting an apartment with some other guys and cooking their own meals.

When Peter told his mother that Virgil was thinking about moving out because she was not cooking like she had agreed to, she said, "I really don't care what he does."

That comment pretty much sealed it for Peter as well, and he decided to move out with Virgil and fend for himself. He could afford to rent an apartment. The rent was cheaper than the dorm fees. He would have to pay for food, but he could manage. Maybe Carrie would take pity on him and feed him. Peter loved his mother and wanted to have a good relationship with her, but he was an adult and wanted to be treated as an adult, and his mother was not doing that. Maybe with him gone from the house, she would miss him and begin to listen to him.

George was at a loss as to what to do about Gladys. He did not want to just let her get more and more depressed and was concerned about her mental health as well as her physical health. The fact that the headaches she was having were not going away was a big worry for him. Somehow, he had to get her to a doctor for a checkup.

Gladys was devastated when Peter moved out. She didn't believe he was serious when he said he would.

"Peter, please. You will not be able to take care of yourself properly if you move out. You need me to cook for you and to do your laundry. Please do not go," Gladys begged.

"Mom, I am 24 years old. I have spent four years in the Navy living on an island in Alaska. I am a sophomore in college. I can take care of myself. I can cook a meal for myself, and I know how to do my own laundry. Please give me some credit?" Peter asked his mother. "Have you changed your mind about Carrie?"

"I am sorry, Peter, but I will not change my mind. She is entirely wrong for you. I know it in my heart and in my bones," Gladys answered. "There is someone better out there for you. Someone who can make you happy. I can find that person for you, Peter. Just give me a chance."

"You have been a good mother, and I appreciate and love you for it. But it is not your job to find me a wife. That is my job, and I have done it, and I think I've done pretty well. I will get married to Carrie Hunter, and we will have children together. I am sorry that you do not approve of her. You will miss out on a good life being a grandmother," Peter stated firmly and walked back to his car to drive away to his own apartment.

Gladys walked back into the house, went to her bedroom, undressed, and went to bed. It was 1:00 o'clock in the afternoon. That is where George found her when he got home from work at 5:30 PM. Again, she had not cleaned up the kitchen from breakfast or lunch, and the living room was a mess. He also noticed that her clothes were strewn all over the floor of the bedroom. She had not picked them up for several days.

"Gladys, wake up!" George said as he shook her to wake her up. "It is too early for you to be in bed. I need to have my dinner, and the house is a mess. You have not cleaned or straightened it up for days."

Gladys opened her eyes and looked at George with an odd look on her face. She was mad at him for bothering her while she was trying to sleep, and she just shoved his hand away from her shoulder.

"My dear, you must get up and start taking care of yourself," George begged. "I need to have you around for a long time, and right now, you are scaring me and making me think you do not care about me or my feelings at all. We have been together for 26 years, and I need to have you around for another 26 at least. Why don't you get up, shower, and dress, and I will take you out to dinner? That would be nice, wouldn't it?"

"Not now, George. I need to sleep right now," Gladys said as she turned over with her back to him.

George felt defeated as he went into the bathroom to wash his face and hands. He headed for the kitchen, but changed his mind and went back to the car and drove to a local tavern for a beer. He ordered a meal of fish and chips and ate it at the bar with another beer, paid for his meal, and went home.

Gladys was still in bed, so George cleaned up the kitchen and went out onto the porch to sit and think. He was tired of doing his job at the mill during the day and having to do Gladys' job when he got home. When he finally went to bed, Gladys was lying with her back to his side of the bed. George usually kissed her goodnight and told her he loved her, but tonight he just got into bed, rolled on his side, and went to sleep.

When George woke up the next morning, Gladys was not in the house or in the yard, but the coffee was brewed in the pot and a cup set out for him. The paper was on the table, and it looked like she had planned on cooking breakfast.

After about a half hour, Gladys came into the kitchen, said good morning to George, and proceeded to start to cook some bacon.

"I have already eaten," George announced. "You were not around, and I need to get to mowing the lawn before the rain starts this afternoon. I had a bowl of cereal."

"I'm sorry. I was going to fix you some bacon and eggs for breakfast. I just took a short walk," Gladys explained.

"You must have taken a long walk. I was up at 6:00 o'clock, and it is now 8:30. You were gone a long time," George countered.

"I'm sorry. I didn't realize I was gone that long," Gladys answered back.

George got up from the table and went out to get the mower out of the shed. He had some big decisions to make as far as Gladys was concerned. On Monday, he was going to call the doctor's office and make an appointment for a complete checkup for her, then he was going to forcibly get her there. He knew that not only was she mentally depressed because of Peter, but he knew that something was physically wrong with her, and he was determined to find out what it was.

On Monday, when he had time between working on the saws, George went into the office to use the phone. He called the doctor's office to make an appointment for Gladys to see the doctor as soon as possible. He made an appointment for Friday at 10 AM and then asked to take Friday off because he had to take his wife to the doctor.

The mill manager was concerned. George had never asked for time off for any reason, and he was never sick. He had not even taken a vacation in the two years he had been working there.

George worked during the day, came home, and fixed himself some supper. Gladys was hardly eating anything and would not get out of bed to fix anything for him. He cleaned up the kitchen, read the paper, and usually went for a short walk before going to bed.

On Friday, George got up, made coffee, and fixed himself some cereal for breakfast, but he did not get ready for work. He put his good slacks and a good shirt on, then told Gladys that she had to get up, get a shower, and dress. They had an appointment with the doctor, and he was not going to take no for an answer.

"Gladys, I will carry you out of this house if I have to, but you are going to see the doctor. You have not been well, and I will not see you waste away without trying to do something about it. Now, get up," George demanded.

Gladys turned over and started to say something to George, but changed her mind. He had a fierce look on his face that she had never seen before. She knew that he would come through with his threat to carry her out of the house if she did not do as he asked.

So, she got out of bed and went into the bathroom to take a shower. George heard the water running and decided not to disturb her while she was showering, but he did not leave the bedroom.

Gladys was hesitant when she came out of the bathroom, but finally dressed. While she was in the shower, George had poured her a cup of coffee and took it to the bedroom for her. She looked at him strangely and nodded her thanks, took a drink, and proceeded to get dressed.

George led her to the car, helped her in, and went around to the driver's side to get in. Gladys had her hand on the door handle when he said to her, "Don't you dare leave this car. We are going to the doctor, and we are going to find out what is wrong with you. At this point, you have no choice."

CHAPTER 18

Gladys was scared. She knew something was wrong with her, but she was afraid to find out. She was ashamed at the way she was acting, but couldn't seem to stop. George was insisting now, and she knew that she could not get out of the appointment.

As George led Gladys into the office, she held back a little, whispering, "I will improve my attitude, George. I will make you dinner every evening and clean up the kitchen, and I will do your laundry again. Just don't make me go in and see the doctor. I am scared."

"You've never been scared of the doctor before. Why now?" George asked.

"I don't know. I just am," she answered.

"Good morning, Mr. and Mrs. Taylor," the doctor said as George and Gladys were escorted into his office. "I am Gerald Kramer. Please, both of you, have a seat." The doctor indicated the two chairs opposite him at his desk.

"Mrs. Taylor, your husband indicated on the phone that you were having increased headaches and that you were tired and somewhat depressed lately. How long has this been going on?" the doctor asked.

"I don't know. For a little over a month, I suppose. Our son told us that he was getting married to a girl that I don't like at all. He will not listen to me when I tell him that she is no good for him. I know what is best for him, but he is determined to make up his own mind," Gladys explained forcefully.

"How old is your son, Mrs. Taylor?" Doctor Kramer asked.

"He is 24 years old," Gladys stated firmly. "He still has a few years of maturing to get through, and he can't do it if he is married to that girl he is seeing," Gladys said with irritation in her voice.

"At his age, I would think that would be his decision. Why do you feel that he is making a mistake?"

"I have a feeling that she is going to make him very unhappy. She is a social climber and will want more than he is willing to give," explained Gladys. "I just don't like her."

"That is your right to dislike anyone. Those are your feelings. The problem is, when you express those opinions to other people, you will alienate them if they don't agree. And obviously, your son does not agree, so he has moved physically away from you so you can't show or express your opinions to him," Dr. Kramer expressed back.

"Now, let's move on to your health concerns. Your husband said that you have obviously been depressed lately, but he also mentioned that you have headaches almost constantly and you are tired all of the time. He says that you are not doing the housework the way you have always done before. Are his observations correct?" the doctor asked.

"George has been talking a lot," Gladys mumbled.

"Is his assessment correct, Mrs. Taylor?" the doctor asked again.

"I suppose so. I haven't felt like cooking or cleaning lately, and yes, I have had headaches. I take an occasional aspirin, but they do no good. Sleep is the only thing that helps," Gladys stated firmly.

When the exam was complete, the doctor asked both Gladys and George to come into his office. As they walked in, Dr. Kramer was just hanging up the phone.

"Mr. Taylor, I want you to take your wife to San Francisco General Hospital for an x-ray of her brain. I believe that she might have some minor bleeding in the brain which, if not halted now, could cause a severe stroke later. Mrs. Taylor, I believe that you have had a minor stroke, probably within the last three weeks. A minor bleed in the brain can cause headaches and tiredness. It would cause you to not be physically able to perform your normal activities. It can also cause you to be irritable and not be your general happy self."

"When do I have to get her there, doctor?" George asked.

"I have just gotten off the phone with them, and they have a time tomorrow at 1:30 in the afternoon. That would give you time to get there and time to get back in the evening. I know it is an inconvenience, but we do not have that kind of x-ray technology in our little hospital as yet, and I feel it is necessary to get a proper diagnosis now before something more serious could occur," Dr. Kramer explained.

"Ok. We will go early tomorrow," George said as he looked at Gladys, whose face was white as a sheet. If she was scared before, she was five times as scared now.

"We will stay in a hotel Friday night and come home on Saturday. We have never been to San Francisco, and I would like to go to Fisherman's Wharf and to see the Golden Gate Bridge," George stated.

"From here, you will drive across the bridge to get into town. My nurse will give you all of the information you will need at the hospital. Mrs. Hunter, please don't be worried. There is no pain involved in the x-ray, and it only takes a few minutes," Doctor Hunter explained.

"Thank you for coming in today. I or my nurse will call you when we get the results from San Francisco General. It usually takes about a week for the radiologist to read and diagnose the x-rays," Dr. Kramer added.

Both George and Gladys were quiet on the drive home. George walked into the house and called Peter to let him know what was happening. "Do you want me to go with you, Dad?" Peter asked.

"I don't think so, son. I want your mother to be as calm as she possibly can be. Right now, your presence might cause her more agitation," George answered his son.

"I have a couple of classes tomorrow, but if I don't answer, Virgil and I have this answering machine hooked up to the phone. Just leave a message, and I will get back to you. And Dad, I love you, and please tell Mom that I love her too," Peter answered.

"Thanks, Peter, and I will tell your mother what you said," George said.

George and Gladys were very quiet on the drive to San Francisco. They had decided to spend the night there and drive back the next day. They were going to do a bit of sightseeing while they were there. As they were driving toward San Francisco on the coast road, they drove through Marin County and all of the little beach towns along the way. It reminded them of Garibaldi and their time on the Oregon Coast. Then they saw the Golden Gate Bridge and were awed by it. They drove across it and marveled at the structure and the fact that they could build a bridge like that over the entrance to San Francisco Bay. They saw Alcatraz Island and the prison built on it and were again amazed at the sight.

The sights were only a minor distraction for them. They were very aware of the reason they were in the city. It did not leave their minds for one second. Gladys was quiet and introspective most of the time. She was scared of the outcome of the x-rays. George did not want to admit it, but he was scared too.

George drove right to the hospital and checked in at the front desk. An orderly came and took Gladys to the x-ray lab while George waited in the main lobby.

It only took about 15 minutes to take the x-rays. Gladys was escorted back to the main lobby where George was, and they were told that Dr. Kramer would receive the results within 3 days. The technician could not give them any information at all.

They decided to try to put it out of their minds for the evening and enjoy themselves. After checking into their hotel, they walked to Fisherman's Wharf for dinner. They each had a great salmon dinner and watched the ships coming and going from the docks. After dinner, they walked back to their hotel and made plans for the next day's sightseeing. Chinatown, Golden Gate Park, the Presidio, and Nob Hill were all on their list of places to see.

George was planning on going home on Saturday afternoon, but they had spent so much time touring the city that it was too late to drive all the way to Arcada, so they stayed another night and headed out the next morning. They drove through the Napa Valley on the way north and admired all of the vineyards, and even stopped at a couple of the wineries.

The weekend proved to have a lot of firsts for the Taylors, but foremost in Gladys' mind was that it was the first time she had ever had x-rays. That was certainly not something that she was excited about. On Monday, Gladys got up with George and fixed his breakfast for him. She hadn't done that for a couple of months.

Gladys was still scared about what was going to happen to her, but a little more comfortable in her own skin now that she had seen a doctor. He was reassuring and did not berate her for not seeing a doctor earlier. She was terribly concerned about someone calling her stupid for delaying the visit to the doctor. She knew she wasn't stupid. It was just very hard for her to put trust in someone she did not know. Her doctor in Missouri she had known all of her life.

George also understood now that Gladys was so scared of what was going on in her own body that she had very little control of her activities. Depression acts like that on some people. They are so deep that they cannot function in their normal manner. The doctor had suggested that she see a professional counselor, but she was not quite ready to confide in someone else.

George had told her that Peter wanted to be a counselor. Maybe she could talk to him.

Peter went over to see Gladys after she returned from San Francisco. He was concerned about her but relieved that she had sought out medical care.

She asked him about seeing him for counseling, but Peter explained to her that he wasn't going to be that kind of counselor. He wanted to be a school counselor and talk to kids about their problems and their futures.

Anyway, it was not a good idea for relatives to practice medicine on their families. They needed someone who was not involved.

Gladys was disappointed but understood why Peter would not be able to be her counselor.

When Gladys found out that Peter could not and would not be her counselor, she decided that she did not need anyone else to talk to. She did not want to talk about her personal life to strangers.

CHAPTER 19

Gladys was trying very hard to be awake and alert during the times that George was home, but she still refused to talk to a professional about her feelings of depression. George knew that she was a very private person, and talking about her personal feelings to him was even difficult for her. She just bottled it up inside.

It was a peaceful Sunday afternoon in October 1954. Gladys was not feeling well, so the Taylors did not go to church that morning. George noticed a kind of gray look to her face while she was sleeping. He bent over, gave her a soft kiss on her cheek, and went to the kitchen to fix himself some breakfast.

He talked to Peter and asked him to come over to see his mother. She was not feeling well, but George knew that a visit from Peter would cheer her up. Peter would not move home again, but he was on pretty good speaking terms with his mother now. As long as they did not speak about Carrie, they were fine.

Gladys was sitting on the sofa in the living room when Peter arrived. She smiled at him and lifted her hand in a gesture asking him to wait a minute. She was listening to the Philharmonic Orchestra on the radio and wanted to hear the end of the symphony.

"What a pleasant surprise," Gladys said as she smiled at Peter. Peter bent over to give her a kiss on the cheek and noticed that her cheek was cold.

"Are you warm enough, Mom?" he asked.

"Sure, I am fine. I have this blanket to keep me warm, and your dad has turned the temperature up on the furnace. The wind was cold outside this morning. How are you?" Gladys asked.

"I'm fine. Very busy right now. Classes seem to be more intense now that I am taking the classes I need to satisfy the requirements of a school counselor. I have books to read, papers to write, and tests to study for. It is a constant thing. I am glad to be able to get away from it for a while to visit you. Sorry I haven't been around much. I have my nose in my books most of the time," Peter explained.

"It sounds very hard. Are you sure that this is the field you want to go into? There must be easier classes to take in other career paths," Gladys speculated.

"I'm sure there are, but this is fascinating to me, and the thought of helping those kids through their young lives gives me a good feeling. I love the idea of helping them, and I love the field of psychology. It is so interesting to me to be able to delve into a person's ideas and thoughts. I don't know very much about it yet, but I will learn," Peter said emphatically.

As he was talking, he noticed that the left side of Gladys' face was sagging a bit. "Mom, are you feeling okay?" he asked.

"Sure, I am fine," Gladys said, but her words were slurred a bit.

Peter jumped up, called his dad in from the kitchen, and said to him, "Dad, call an ambulance right away. I think Mom is having a stroke."

George rushed to the phone and dialed the operator to get an ambulance to the house. Peter went back to Gladys, and she had a stunned look on her face.

"Peter, I don't feel very good. Will you help me to bed, please?" she mumbled to him.

"Mama, Dad has called an ambulance. You need to go to the hospital. I think you are having a stroke. The ambulance will come and get you to the hospital very quickly. You will be fine," Peter told her very hopefully.

"I don't want to go to the hospital. I don't like those places," Gladys whispered. Peter and George could barely hear or understand her.

The ambulance came, loaded Gladys into the back, and took off with the sirens blaring. George and Peter climbed into Peter's car and raced after it.

Gladys indeed did have a stroke, but Peter recognized the symptoms right away and was able to get her immediate help. She was in the hospital for almost a month, then went to a rehabilitation facility where she could get intensive therapy for her left side and for her speech. She was working hard on both her speech and arm and leg movements. Having her speech affected caused her to forget words, but she was getting better daily and looking forward to the day she would come home.

George was also looking forward to that day. He was coping with cooking his own meals, doing the laundry, and cleaning the house all the while working and visiting Gladys every day. He was exhausted. Some of the ladies from church offered to help with the housework, but George knew that Gladys would not like that at all, so he refused the help. Peter came over when he could to give a little help with the cleaning, but most of his time was taken up with studying and being with Carrie. He did manage a ten to fifteen minute visit with his mother about every other day. Having Gladys away was hard on both George and Peter.

The neighbors were very good about making sure that George had plenty to eat. He had to refuse some of the food that was offered. He had too much and could not eat it all. Sometimes he would take meals to Gladys so they could eat together, but she had a hard time getting food to her mouth and was embarrassed to let people see her eat, even George. She was grateful that George understood her feelings and didn't mind that she did not want to eat with him. She was grateful for the food, though. She didn't like the food at the rehab center.

Peter and Carrie had been talking about a wedding date before Gladys had her stroke, but now everything was on hold. Carrie wanted Peter to go back to Kansas with her over Christmas to meet her family, but even that was on hold. Because of the way Gladys felt about Carrie and her own fragile health, Peter was reluctant to leave. He would never forgive himself if something happened to her and he was gone. Carrie understood and was very sympathetic to his situation. She wanted to be friends with Gladys but did not know how to get around the dislike that Gladys had for her. She did not understand why she felt that way. Peter tried to explain to her that Gladys was always very possessive of him and didn't even want him to spend time alone with his dad. Carrie did not understand that feeling at all. Her family was open and loving toward all members of the family and didn't have a jealous bone in their bodies.

Carrie had decided that she was going to go home for Christmas even if Peter couldn't go with her. She wanted to spend time with her parents and her brothers and sisters before she was married.

Carrie's parents were disappointed that Peter was not coming with their daughter for the holiday, but understood that his mother was very ill and he did not want to be away. Carrie wanted to get married in California, so they would have to wait to meet him until they arrived the week before the wedding. They had talked to him on the phone, so felt that they knew him a little at least.

Carrie and Peter were planning a June 1954 wedding. School would be out, and Peter would have some time for a short honeymoon. They both wanted to drive down to Big Sur, stopping at Carmel and Monterey along the way. Carrie would be able to take a week off for the trip.

The ceremony itself would be small and held at 10 AM. George had told them that he would be pleased to take them all out to lunch afterward. Peter was only hoping that Gladys would be able and willing to attend.

The rehab facility that Gladys was in was allowing her to come home on the weekends now to see how she coped. She had a walker that she used around the house to give her support in walking. Unfortunately, the house was not built to accommodate a wheelchair, so she was not able to use one inside. Her attendance at the wedding was still up in the air.

"George, I don't really want to attend the wedding. I am so against it that I am afraid I will say something I shouldn't," Gladys said. It was one of the longest sentences she had spoken so far and took great effort on her part. She was still having trouble talking and forming sentences.

"You know Peter will be very disappointed if you are not there," George answered.

"No one will miss me. All of the attention will be paid to Carrie and her family."

"Believe me, Gladys, you will be missed, and there's no reason you need to be embarrassed. You have been ill, and everyone understands that. Anyway, the wedding isn't for another 2 months. You will be much better by then," George told her, trying to encourage her to work hard and get better.

"I will think about it," answered Gladys.

CHAPTER 20

Gladys was glad to be home. She wasn't able to do any of her usual household chores, and George had to help her dress in the morning. She used a walker to get around the house, and sometimes George found her just wandering from one room to the other without seeming to have a purpose for being in the room. He supposed that it was good exercise for her to get up and walk. The weather wasn't very conducive to walking outside now, and Gladys didn't want anyone to see her hobbling around.

George was exhausted most of the time. He was working his full-time job at the mill along with taking care of Gladys in the morning and evening. A paid practical nurse came in five days a week while George was at work. She helped bathe Gladys and take care of a lot of her physical needs.

George thanked God every day that the mill had good health insurance for their employees. He still had a lot of money going out, but at least most of the cost was covered.

Every sound that Gladys made at night woke George up. He was afraid that she would have another stroke and he wouldn't hear her. Peter would come over in the evening sometimes and bring dinner. Carrie was a good cook and would fix extra for

George and Gladys. Peter didn't tell Gladys that it was from Carrie. She would not have accepted it if she knew. It was only a month before the wedding, and Gladys had yet to decide if she was going. She would need a new dress if she was, but she wouldn't make up her mind for sure.

One evening in early May, Gladys was sitting on the sofa listening to the Boston Pops Orchestra when she turned to George and said, "George, you have been a good husband. I love you." At that moment, she leaned her head back and was no longer breathing.

George jumped up from his chair and ran to her, yelling for her to wake up, but she was dead. George didn't often cry, but he had huge racking sobs at the loss of his wife. He sat on the sofa holding her for about ten minutes, then realized that he had to call Peter. He laid Gladys down on the sofa, put a blanket over her, and went to call Peter.

Peter was with Carrie when the phone rang. He answered it. When he realized it was his dad, he asked, "What's wrong, Dad? Is Mom okay?"

"Your mama is dead, Peter. She died about fifteen minutes ago. Do you want to see her before I call the ambulance to take her away?" George asked his son.

"I will be right there. Don't do anything, Dad. I will take care of it. Please, sit down and try to stay calm. I will be there soon."

When Peter arrived at his parents' home, Carrie was with him. She called the ambulance and went in to put a pot of coffee on the stove.

Peter and George tried to console each other, but were doing a poor job of it. They had both argued with Gladys and knew that she was a difficult person to live with, but they both loved her so much, and life would not be the same without her.

The ambulance came and took Gladys to the morgue. George had requested no autopsy. He already knew what had caused her death.

Peter and Carrie stayed at the house that night. Peter wasn't about to leave his dad alone.

Carrie naturally thought about the wedding. She wondered if she was going to have to postpone the ceremony. She hoped not. Her parents were taking the train from Kansas, and their plans were already made. She would call them tomorrow.

Peter was in a state of shock, but able to function and take care of necessary arrangements that had to be made. He had called his uncles and let them know about Gladys' death. All of them were coming to the funeral. They wanted to pay their respects to their brother and to make sure that he was okay. Maybe they didn't see each other very often or talk all the time, but they all loved each other and cared very much for each other's well-being.

The funeral service would be at eleven on a Saturday morning, and the ladies of the church were planning a lunch afterward. George knew that a bunch of people would come to the house afterward, so he hired some ladies to come in and clean. He didn't feel comfortable having family or friends clean his house.

The funeral service was dignified and fairly brief. Neither George nor Peter wanted a long, drawn-out affair with people getting bored and fidgeting in their seats.

The service was perfect afterward. George didn't eat much, and Peter was worried about him, but he insisted he was fine, just tired. He had not had a good night's sleep since Gladys died. Things would settle down soon.

After about a week, George went back to work. He was tired just sitting around the house mourning Gladys. There were times when she was difficult to live with, but she had been a good wife and mother, and he loved her and missed her very much.

Carrie and Peter's wedding was a beautiful event that brought a little joy into George's world. He was able to spend time with Carrie's family, and they greeted him and accepted him into their family with grace and kindness. He felt welcome. He sorely missed Gladys' presence, but knew that it would not have been a happy time for her, and he was sorry for that. She could have had a good relationship with the Hunter family. They were very nice, down-to-earth people, and George enjoyed their company and getting to know them.

George was never sorry that he brought his family to the West. It was the best move that he could have made at the time. He was only sorry that Gladys was not happy. She always missed Missouri and her farm life.

George now had some decisions to make about his life. Even though Peter and Carrie were planning to stay in Arcada until he graduated, their plans were uncertain after that. Peter knew he had to continue with school and get his master's degree before he could get a job in the counseling field, but he was uncertain where he would go. George did not really want to stay in California. He wanted to be closer to his brothers. He thought he might like to be in Portland, near Charles, Gwen, and the babies. Another son had been born last year, and he had not met him yet.

"I think I will probably move to Portland to be near Charlie and his family," George mentioned to Peter and Carrie one Sunday afternoon. "I am not really tied to anything here. I have enough money to live for a while without working, and I can always pick up a temp job if I need to. I might even travel a bit. I would like to see Yellowstone Park and the surrounding area. What do you think about that idea?"

"It's great, Dad! We will only be here for another eight months and will probably go to Seattle and the University of Washington for my post-graduate work, so if you are based in Portland, we would be fairly close," Peter commented.

"George, you need to do something for yourself," Carrie added. "You had a long haul taking care of and worrying about Gladys. It is time for you to relax and think about yourself for a change. I know you miss her, but take time to enjoy life. As we all know, it is uncertain what will happen to any of us. Travel, see what you want to see. Meet new people. Have a good time."

George turned in his resignation to the manager of the mill on Monday. He gave them a two-week notice so that they could find another filer. He called Charlie and Gwen to let them know his plans and check to see if he could stay there for a while. He called a realtor and put his house up for sale. When all was set, he gave a lot of his furniture to Peter and Carrie. They had very little of their own, and they were grateful to have it. He packed up the rest of his stuff and put it in a storage locker. Carrie and Peter would bring it north with them when they moved to Seattle. George would sort through it then. It was still too soon after Gladys passed to go through a lot of her things.

On August 8th, just a few days after George's 57th birthday, he signed the papers on the sale of his house, got in his car, and headed north. He was going to drive up the Pacific Coast Highway to Garibaldi to visit the Greens and the Johnsons, then head into Portland to Charlie and Gwen's house.

New adventures awaited George Taylor. He missed his wife and wished she had lived long enough to enjoy these times with him, but he was looking forward to his new life and future.

The End